The Missing Librarian

Satanik Basu

Ukiyoto Publishing

All global publishing rights are held by

Ukiyoto Publishing

Published in 2023

Content Copyright © Satanik Basu

ISBN 9789360169701

All rights reserved.
No part of this publication may be reproduced, transmitted, or stored in a retrieval system, in any form by any means, electronic, mechanical, photocopying, recording or otherwise, without the prior permission of the publisher.

The moral rights of the author have been asserted.

This is a work of fiction. Names, characters, businesses, places, events, locales, and incidents are either the products of the author's imagination or used in a fictitious manner. Any resemblance to actual persons, living or dead, or actual events is purely coincidental.

This book is sold subject to the condition that it shall not by way of trade or otherwise, be lent, resold, hired out or otherwise circulated, without the publisher's prior consent, in any form of binding or cover other than that in which it is published.

www.ukiyoto.com

Acknowledgement

My love and attraction towards detective stories were from my childhood. As I am a Bengali language speaker, I started with "Feluda" a Bengali detective written by the great Satyajit Ray. As I grew up, slowly Sherlock Holmes, Hercule Poirot, Miss Marple, Byomkesh (another Bengali detective) and many more detective characters entered my life. But the four detective characters that made impact in my life were Feluda, Sherlock Holmes, Hercule Poirot and Byomkesh. I never thought that I will write a book and create my own detective character. So, as I started writing, I kept in mind everything about my favourite detective writers and characters. The story is set in 1950's England. I'm strictly against the use of artificial intelligence in detective stories. So, this story doesn't have the use of any technology. This is the simple case of detection and deduction. In the words of the great "Hercule Poirot", using of the "little grey cells". I hope all the readers will love and enjoy this story.

And in the end a huge thanks to Ukitiyo Publishing. I am so much grateful to them. Without their help this story would have never been published. Thanks Ukitiyo Publishing for this wonderful opportunity.
Satanik Basu

Contents

A Strange Incident	1
An Unsettling Peace	22
The Long-Haired Man	36
Two Deaths and a Detective	54
The Painter	82
Two Alphabets	97
The Man from the Petrol Pump	115
Three Bullets and a Man Down	136
The Meeting	153
Too Much Cunning Overreaches Itself	163
About the Author	*181*

A Strange Incident

"Dorothy, please come to my office" Harold Carter said Carter.

Dorothy was talking to a reader of the library. She said—

"Give me five minutes Sir."

Harold Carter was looking a little anxious. Dorothy went into his office room five minutes later. She looked at Harold Carter and asked—

"Everything is alright Sir? You are looking a little tense."

"Where is the book 'At the villa Rose written by A.W.E Mason'?" Harold Carter asked.

"It is right where it should be. Why Sir?" Dorothy asked.

"Well, it is not there. Go and take a look at yourself" Harold Carter said.

"Strange. But I distinctly remember Sir I kept the book there myself" Dorothy said.

"Do you remember who was reading it?" Harold Carter asked.

"A young gentleman Sir, name Paul Collins" Dorothy said.

"Are you sure about that exact same book I am talking about? You could have kept some other book" Harold Carter said.

"I am sure Sir. It was 'At the villa Rose'. I remember it very well because the gentleman who was reading the book was asking to borrow it back home. He was very keen to complete the novel today. It was the same book you are talking about Sir" Dorothy said.

"Jesus Christ. It happened again" Harold said, shaking his head.

"What happened Sir? Is everything alright?" Dorothy asked.

"Oh! Certainly, my dear. Nothing to worry about. Everything is alright. You carry on" Harold Carter said.

Dorothy left with a suspicious face. Harold Carter stood there for a few more minutes before sitting on his chair. She was on her way to her office room when she remembered something about the book. So, she went back to Harold Carter's office.

"May I come in Sir?" Dorothy asked.

"Yes. Come in" Harold Carter said.

"I forgot to tell you Sir; Madam Julia was going through the pages of that book after I kept it there. You may ask her" Dorothy said.

"Thank you very much Dorothy. You may go now and please send Julia in here" Harold Carter said.

"Right away Sir" Dorothy said and left Harold Carter's office.

Julia Wilson is the Secretary of the library. Harold Carter's father built this library twenty years ago. Now Harold Carter is running the library in his father's absence. The library had a different name when his father was alive. But after his death Harold Carter named the library after his father J.C. Library. This library is one of the oldest libraries in London. It is near Regent's park.

Julia Wilson came a few minutes later.

"You were looking for me?" she asked.

"Do you know where the book 'At the villa Rose' is? Yesterday Dorothy put the book herself. You were going through the book afterwards. Well, it is not there anymore. Can you tell me where it is?" Harold Carter asked.

"Well, just like Dorothy, I too put it there Harold" Julia Wilson said.

"Then where has it gone? A book can't vanish itself, can it?" Harold Carter asked.

"I think someone else must have kept it elsewhere. Don't think about this too much" Julia Wilson said.

Then she looked towards Harold Carter for few seconds and said—

"How about I come tonight to your home? We haven't spent a night together for a long time, have we?"

"Well, it will be wonderful if you would come" Harold Carter said and then he kissed Julia Wilson.

"Not here my love. Someone will see us" Julia Wilson said.

"Only Dorothy is here darling and she is upstairs in her office. So, I think no one is here to see us" Harold Carter said and then he kissed her again. This time a little longer.

"I am leaving my love. And don't bother to cook. I will bring our dinner" Julia Wilson said while leaving.

"Don't be late" Harold Carter said.

He was happy. Indeed, they are going to spend a night after a long time but that matter with the book wasn't going out of Harold Carter's head. It was five pasts thirty in the evening. The library closes at five o clock. Harold Carter is always the last person to leave. Before leaving the library, he goes to every room to check whether everything is in order or not. It was 5.35 pm when he left the library.

The distance between Harold Carter's house and the library is not too far. It is a twenty minutes' walk. So, most of the time Harold Carter goes to the library by walking. But now he wasn't feeling like going home. So, he decided to go to Regent's park instead of going home. The Regent's Park falls in between his house and his library. He went inside the park and sat on a bench beside a young fellow.

"Are you alright Sir?" asked the young fellow sitting beside Harold Carter.

"Oh, certainly young man. I am absolutely alright" Harold Carter said.

"But you don't seem alright. Your face is a little paled" said the young fellow again.

"Well, I believe that is because of my age. As you can see, I am pretty old to look handsome. There is nothing to worry about, my son. I am fine. And by the way, thank you for asking. You can carry on" Harold Carter said.

The young fellow said "You must be Mr Harold Carter, right?"

Harold Carter was a little surprised to hear that. He couldn't remember how that young fellow knew him. He asked—

"Do I know you from somewhere?"

"You don't know me Sir. But I do. My name is Paul Collins. I am a member of your library," said the young fellow.

"Paul Collins?" Harold Carter muttered himself. The name seemed familiar to him. And soon he remembered. He said—

"You were the one who was reading the book 'At the villa Rose'? Weren't you?"

"Yes Sir. I wanted to complete the book tonight, Sir. That's why I asked Madam Dorothy to lend me the book. But she denied," said Paul Collins.

"Yes, she told me about that. But we don't lend books to our readers anymore because of some incidents that happened in the past. But it is wonderful to see a young man like you have chosen to be a member of a library" Harold Carter said.

"Thank you, Sir," said Paul Collins.

"Are you waiting for someone son?" Harold Carter asked.

"Ah, yes Sir. I am waiting for my lover," said Paul Collins.

"I see. And what is the name of that beautiful lady?" Harold Carter asked.

"Her name is Doris, Sir. I should be going. She will be waiting at the gate," said Paul Collins.

"Don't keep her waiting. Be hurry" Harold Carter said with a smile.

Harold Carter was still sitting on the bench. A strange stir was going on in his mind. Something seems wrong. There is something happening in the library. He had this doubt so many times in the last few months. But he had no proof. He still doesn't have any proof. It's been 12 years now that he is working in the J.C. library. He began as a normal librarian under his father but eventually became the chief librarian and the owner of the library after his father's death. He is unmarried but he loves Julia Wilson. They are in a relationship with each other for the last six years. Harold Carter even proposed to her a few times now for marriage. But Julia Wilson declined his proposal every time. She is happy with the way everything is going on. Harold Carter has a passion for books. He devoted his whole life to books. He believes that books are the doorway to the new world. The knowledge and wisdom we receive from books will help us to turn this world into a better place. But now a black shadow has created an obstacle in the path of knowledge and wisdom. And he is determined to uncover this mystery. He doesn't know yet what it is. But he can guess that whatever is going on inside that library is not ethical and definitely not legal either. The young fellow Paul Collins, with whom Harold Carter was talking to a while ago, almost understood that he is going through some stress. Paul Collins tried to reach Harold Carter's mind. Because he doubted something was wrong. But Harold Carter did well. He didn't let Paul Collins understand what he was thinking. But he can't let this happen anymore. He has to be more contained about this matter. Otherwise, everyone will understand by his facial expression that he is going through something. Something, which is not allowing him to have a sound sleep at night. A doubt which is constantly bothering him. He noticed this matter a few months back when a book suddenly disappeared from the library. And just like it disappeared, it came back in the same way a few days later. And this incident kept repeating itself thereafter. And every time he thought that the matter was getting serious and decided to report a theft, the books used to come back mysteriously and were kept exactly where they should be. He wasn't able to solve this mystery. He had spoken with each and every member and worker of his library including Julia Wilson. But nothing came out. Since then, he stays worried all the time.

"Something has to be done" Harold Carter tells himself, stood up and started walking towards his home. He tried to stay normal. Because on his way back he will meet some people he knows.

Julia Wilson came around eight o'clock in the evening. She cooked Harold Carter's favourite food. It has been a while since they had dinner together. Harold Carter's relationship with Julia Wilson is a little complicated. Though they have known each other for the last six years, there is something strange in their relationship. They love each other very much but they never get along like every other couple do. For some exceptional reason Julia Wilson does not want to marry Harold Carter. Harold Carter is a wonderful man. He is honest and courageous. Though he is forty-two years old, he looks a little younger than his actual age. He is also wealthy. So, there must be an unusual reason why Julia Wilson was declining his marriage proposal. Julia was arranging dinner on the dining table. Harold Carter was sitting on a chair near the window. He seemed a little distracted. That caught Julia's eye.

"What's the matter my love?" Julia Wilson asked.

"Nothing my dear. Let's eat" Harold Carter said and they both sat down to eat at the dining table.

After eating they both went into the bedroom. Harold was still distracted.

"Is something bothering you? You seem a little distracted from the time I arrived here" Julia asked.

Harold said "I told you little dove. It's nothing."

"Little dove? What happened to the darling?" Julia asked, smiling.

"I thought it would be appropriate. That's why I said it" Harold Carter said.

"Everything will be appropriate for me my love once you start to love me" Julia Wilson said and then she opened her clothes.

Harold pulled Julia towards him and then began to kiss her and Julia responded with everything she had. In the perfection of love, two bodies became one. With every kiss of Harold Julia felt heavenly bliss. His love for Julia was more than real. And after this wonderful moment they slept the rest of the night holding each other.

In the morning when Harold woke up, Julia was already gone. She left a letter for her love on the dining table. Harold read the letter, smiled and kissed. It was a drawing of a heart with Harold's name in the middle of it. He was very happy. After a long time, he spent such a wonderful night with Julia. All the distraction, tension from yesterday had already gone out of the window. He felt the morning like a new beginning.

Well, every time he spent a night with Julia, the next morning always seemed like a new beginning to him. After a wonderful bath and cherishing breakfast, Harold left for the library. He seemed like an entirely new man to everyone. The newspaper seller, the wine cellar, all of them were looking at Harold Carter with a lot of surprise. He got the same look from Dorothy until she reminded him of the incident going in the library.

"Oh, dear God. Is there happiness for a moment?" Harold said with frustration.

Dorothy was stunned. She didn't understand what to do.

"What happened Sir? Did you forget what is happening here? Did I say anything wrong?" Dorothy asked in fear.

"No Dorothy. You have nothing to do with this. Actually, I spent a wonderful time with Julia Wilson yesterday. You know how charming she is. She made me forget all of these. Alright, you were saying something" Harold Carter said.

Dorothy said "Sir, something strange is happening in the library. I also noticed the disappearance of the books but I didn't care then. I do now, especially after what I saw last night."

"Last night?" Dorothy's words took Harold by shock. "What did you see last night? And where?" He asked.

"Right here Sir. I was standing on the street." Dorothy said.

Harold shook his head in anger.

"You were here last night? Alone?" he asked.

"Yes Sir" Dorothy said. She was looking at the floor.

"What time was it?" Harold Carter asked.

"Half past twelve Sir" she replied in a very low voice.

"Have you gone mad Dorothy? Do you have any idea how dangerous it was? Anything could have happened to you. Maybe the war has ended but it will still take some time to settle down. Anyway, what did you see?" Harold Carter asked.

Dorothy said "everything you said yesterday was swirling in my head. I kept on thinking about the matter. It is not possible for a book to disappear itself unless someone is doing this on purpose. And if you noticed Sir, all the disappearance happened after the library was closed. That means it happened at night when no one was inside the library. So, I decided to visit the place at night alone. Though I didn't go inside, I was still sure I would see something. And I did. I distinctly remember I turned off all the lights of the first floor before leaving. But when I arrived there, I saw a glimpse of light the second floor. It was immediately turned off after turning on. At first, I thought there was something illusive about my sight. So, I went inside the gate for a closer look. It happened again. And then I saw the light of a torch. The light was moving around the bookshelves. And all of these were happening on the second floor in room number 21. Someone was there Sir with a very bad purpose. Whatever is happening there is illegal Sir."

Harold was stunned by silence listening to her words.

"But who will do this?" Harold asked with a lot of questions in his eyes.

"Do you think any of our readers are doing this? Because we stopped lending the books. So, they are coming at night like a thief, stealing the books and returning them after a few days when they finished reading. Isn't this possible Dorothy?" he asked again.

"Definitely possible Sir but isn't this becoming a little obvious? I don't know Sir if this is the work of one of our readers or someone else's, but by no means is whatever is happening right. I think you should talk to Madam Julia about this. This is turning into a serious matter now" Dorothy said.

"Hmm" Harold nodded his head and then said "do you really believe this is not the work of one of our readers?" He asked.

"No Sir" Dorothy said.

"And why is that?" Harold Carter asked.

"Sir, every member of our library is honest and true to their nature. I can guarantee you that. I think you already know this by now. That's why I don't think any one of them is doing this. This is the work of someone else with a very bad purpose" Dorothy said.

"If not the members, then who? Look Dorothy it is not possible for an outsider to do this. Whoever is doing this must be from inside. Maybe any of the workers are involved. But I don't understand one thing. Why on earth would someone steal books? And to be honest, you cannot pronounce this stealing because whoever is doing this, is also returning the books after a few days. I mean why would somebody do this unless you want to read it? Why should somebody break into a library and steal books for a few days? Ah! All these seemed to get more complicated. Anyway, have you told anyone else about your last night's adventure?" Harold Carter asked.

Dorothy said "No Sir. Because I don't know who to trust except you and Madam Julia."

"Alright, I'll talk to Julia about this. If necessary, I will go to the police but you will never ever go out alone in the night again. Do you hear me, Dorothy?" Harold Carter said with authority.

"I beg a pardon for my last night's activity Sir. It won't happen again" Dorothy said and left the room.

Harold sat on the chair with a load of thought inside his head. This matter is eating him from inside. He really needs to speak to Julia about this matter. So, he decided to speak to Julia today about this matter after library hours. He went to Julia's office room but the door was closed. Harold was a little surprised. Julia should have arrived by now. It was half past eleven in the morning. She is never late. It was already one hour late from her actual arrival time. So, he decided to visit

Julia's place. He knocked the door of Dorothy's office room and said—

"Dorothy, it's me, Harold."

"Oh, please come in Sir. So sorry Sir, I forgot to keep the door open" Dorothy said.

"It is alright Dorothy. Julia hasn't arrived yet which is a little unusual. I will go down to her house and check on her. I will come back within an hour" Harold Carter said.

Dorothy said "I hope she is alright Sir."

"Me too Dorothy" Harold Carter said and then left for Julia Wilson's house.

Julia Wilson's house was a little far from the library. She lives in Chiswell Street. So, Harold decided to take his car. It took Harold thirty fifty minutes to reach Julia's house. When Harold reached her house, she was sitting in her drawing room. She was surprised to see Harold there.

"What a pleasant surprise. What are you doing here?" Julia asked.

Harold said "Why didn't you come to the library. I thought you must be ill. So, I came to check on you."

"Oh, my love. I am alright. Nothing happened to me. It was just a headache and wasn't going away. So, I thought let's stay home today. But you could have sent anyone else instead of coming here. Don't you have a library to run?" Julia asked.

"I was worried about you Julia. That's why I have come. And I can't send anyone else to check on my lover. It has to be me because you are mine and mine only" Harold Carter said.

Julia Wilson looked at Harold, kissed her and said "Well, as you are already here, let's eat lunch together. What do you say?"

"Ah, my darling, it is a wonderful idea. Though I told Dorothy I am coming back within an hour, it's alright if I am late. She knows about us" Harold Carter said.

Julia said "Darling, the whole library knows about us."

Harold and Julia had a good time again. They spoke about a lot of things over their lunch. But Harold never brought up the topic of what he thought he would speak with Julia. Before leaving Julia's place Harold was looking around the house when he found a list in her study table. A list of book names. Harold trembled after reading the paper. Julia was still in the kitchen. He put the paper into his pocket and went to the kitchen to tell Julia that he is getting late and he has to go. He came back to the library two hours later. As he was about to get off from his car, he spotted a piece of paper on the back seat of the car. He picked up the piece of paper. There was something written on it which shook his entire body for a moment. He was terrified about what was written on the paper. His face became pale again. He knows what this means.

"Dorothy was right" he said to himself. His hands were shaking. And right then the young member of the library Paul Collins was about to go inside the library. Before he could ask anything to Harold, Harold said to him—

"Paul, can you kindly tell Dorothy Burton that I am not feeling well and I am leaving for today? I should take rest. Tell her to come to my home after closing the library. She has the key of the library. Can you do that for me?"

"Of course, Sir. Why not? But is it anything serious? In that case you may need a doctor" Paul said.

Harold put his hand on Paul's shoulder, smiled and said—

"There is no need for a doctor, Paul. It is just a headache. It will be alright after a nap, I guess. You are a good lad, Paul. Stay like this throughout your life. Alright, off you go." Harold went inside his car and drove straight to his home.

Harold spent the afternoon restlessly. It was that piece of paper which was causing all the trouble. Normally Harold doesn't drink a lot but today he finished a whole bottle of whiskey. He couldn't decide what he should do. Dorothy came in the evening. By the time Harold was fully drunk. He opened the door somehow.

"Paul said you were not feeling well. I think you should…. Jesus Christ. Are you drunk? What happened Sir?" Dorothy was shocked. Because she knows Harold doesn't drink much.

Harold sat down on a chair and started weeping. Dorothy almost ran towards him and asked helplessly—

"What's going on Sir? Why are you weeping? What happened? At least I can help you."

Harold took a little time to get back to normal again. Then he handed Dorothy the piece of paper he found in Julia's study table.

Dorothy read the paper and said "There is nothing written here except the names of some books. Why are you so upset about it?"

Harold said "These are the books which disappeared in the last few months and then eventually came back."

Dorothy's eyes become widened. She read the paper again and asked "where did you get this?"

Harold said "in Julia's house. It was kept in her study table."

"What? Impossible" Dorothy almost screamed.

"Do you think I am joking Dorothy? That's the woman I love. Why would I doubt her if there is nothing to doubt? It was kept on her study table. I was shocked the way you are shocked right now" Harold said these last few words with anguish and then he handed another piece of paper to Dorothy which he found inside his car.

"'Stay out of whatever is happening in the library. Don't try to contact the police. Else you will be dead'".

My god. It is a threat" Dorothy said in a frightened voice.

"I found this in the back of my car. It wasn't there when I left the library. I found it when I was about to get out of the car after coming back from Julia's house. You were right Dorothy. Something illegal is going on and if Julia is doing this, then she knows that we know about this matter but I don't think that she believes that I am doubting her. That's why she sent me this threat letter" Harold Carter said.

Dorothy said "This handwriting is not Madam Julia's. I know that for sure. Then how do you know she is involved?" Dorothy asked.

Harold said "Maybe she is not alone. She has more people involved in this. She didn't write me this threat letter because why would she take the risk of revealing herself to me? She is too clever to do that. I know her. She is cunning and smart. Tell me Dorothy, why was this book list in Julia's study room? These are the exact books that disappeared. This can't be a coincidence. She could have written more names but she didn't. Why? She is involved Dorothy."

"Just a minute Sir. Even if I believe you for a moment and think that she is involved, then tell me Sir, why did she leave that book list on her study table? So that you can find it? You said to yourself that she is not foolish. So if she is involved, then why did she take a risk like that?" Dorothy asked.

Harold said "I think she did it by mistake. Like I said, she knows that I know about the matter but she also knows that I don't doubt her. And not only that, she also didn't expect me at her house earlier today. She thought I was in the library. And even if I would come to see why she didn't go to the library that would have been after the library hours. By then she would have hidden that book list somewhere. She didn't think I was coming that early. That's why she kept the book list there. She left my house this morning before I even woke up. Why was she in such a hurry?"

Dorothy seems puzzled. She stood still for a minute and then said—

"But by now she definitely has found out that you have taken the booklist?" Dorothy asked.

"May be. But somehow, I have to convince her that I didn't take it" Harold said.

"What will you do now? Will you go to the police? It will be risky. Because they will not take one book list and a threat letter as a solid proof. They may say that someone made fun of you by sending that letter." Dorothy's voice was shivering.

"Yes, I will go to the police but not now. I need proof before I take any steps. The police will not believe me if I say that books are disappearing and coming back after a few days automatically. They will laugh. Look Dorothy, we have to behave normally in front of Julia. Or she will doubt both of us. We can't let her know that we are watching her. And if your words are true

Dorothy, then definitely she has found out that the book list is missing." Harold Carter said.

Then he started weeping again. "I gave her everything Dorothy. I loved her with everything I have. And still she betrayed me. Oh god, I can't tolerate this anymore. Go home Dorothy. I will be alright. I have to be. I just need a little bit of time. Good night, Dorothy."

"Good night, Sir." As Dorothy was about to leave, she heard a noise.

"What's that?" she asked.

"What?" Harold asked.

"Didn't you hear something? I think I heard the sound of glass being broken. It came from the drawing room. Wait here. Let me see" Dorothy said and went to the drawing room.

She came trembling with a piece of paper in her hand. She said—

"Someone threw this through the window wrapping it with a stone. That's the sound I heard. It has the same handwriting just as the threat letter has Sir."

Harold almost snatched the paper from Dorothy.

"Stop doing your own investigation. I will not harm you unless you do something silly. And don't inform the police. Otherwise, there will be consequences." Harold read and then sat on the chair.

"Oh my God. What will you do Sir?" there was a sign of fear in Dorothy's voice.

"I have to investigate this. I need to go to the library at night. I have to see with my own eyes what is going on there. I can't let this happen. And I also need more proof to prove whether Julia is involved or not. I have to go alone" Harold said.

"Please don't go, Sir. This can be dangerous" Dorothy said. She was worried.

"Don't worry Dorothy. I will be alright. But I am not going tonight or tomorrow. If I need your help, I will tell you. But for now, I want to stay alone. Just go home Dorothy" Harold said.

"Alright Sir. I think you should take a break from the library. I and Madam Julia will take good care of it. I don't know what you are thinking and I also don't care what those letters say but I truly believe that Madam Julia is not involved in all of this and I believe this from the bottom of my heart. You need to think thoroughly, Sir. But for the sake of your relationship, please say nothing to Madam Julia unless you get solid proof. I beg of you Sir. Because if she gets to know that you are doubting her for this matter, she will be immensely hurt. Please say nothing to her" Dorothy said.

"I won't Dorothy. Now please leave me alone."

Dorothy stood there for a minute or so and then left the house slowly.

An Unsettling Peace

Julia Wilson was reading a newspaper sitting on a chair in her drawing room. It was half past nine in the morning on the clock. Normally by this time Julia reaches the library. But today she was a little stressed. The day before yesterday was wonderful. Because after a long time she spent a good quality time with Harold. But in all of these wonderful moments one thing is still poking Julia's mind. The distracted face of Harold. Throughout the night Harold was distracted even during their romantic moments. But eventually she succeeded in bringing back the man she loves.

But the next day when Harold came to her house to see her, there was a shadow of tension on Harold's face. Julia could see it. And the strangest thing of all, Harold left Julia's house in a hurry which was still a mystery to Julia till last night. But now everything has started to make sense. Now Julia has begun to realise what is going on with Harold. The book list has gone missing. Did Harold see that? Has he taken it with him? How much does he know about Julia's involvement behind the disappearances of the books? All these questions were circling in Julia's mind. So, she decided to talk to him to know whether Harold knows about the matter or not. But she has to be clever. She can't ask directly. She looked at the clock. It was 9:40. Harold should be in the library now.

Julia Wilson took her car and drove straight to the library. But Harold was not in his office. So went to Dorothy's office and asked her—

"Good morning, Dorothy. Harold is not in his office. Didn't he come yet? It is almost 10:30."

"No Madam. He was feeling a little sick yesterday. He also left the library earlier. I went to his house last evening to see if he was alright or not. He wasn't Madam. He was drinking a lot when reached his house. You know he doesn't drink a lot. Something is wrong with him. But he told me nothing of the matter. I think you should talk to him. He is in his house. I advised him not to come today and assured him that me and you will take good care of his library" Dorothy said.

Julia smiled, hugged Dorothy and said—

"It is so kind of you that you went to see him yesterday and told him to stay home Dorothy. I always tell Harold that he is very lucky to have such a wonderful person like you. Thank you, Dorothy."

Julia came out of Dorothy's office with a hundred percent surety that Harold knows. She went straight to Harold's home.

Harold was standing outside his home when Julia reached his house. She was a bit surprised to see him outside of his home at that particular time.

"Harold? What are you doing?" Julia asked.

Harold was startled by Julia's voice. He turned around and saw Julia standing behind him with a lot of questions in her face. Harold was shocked to see Julia there. Because he wasn't expecting her then.

"Julia. Goodness gracious me. OH. I was about to have a heart attack. What are you doing here? I thought you would be in the library" Harold said.

"I went to the library darling. But Dorothy said that you are ill and took today off. So, I came to see you. My God Harold. What happened to you? Did you take a look at yourself in the mirror? Just look at your face. You didn't sleep last night, right? And why were you drinking? Just see what you have done to yourself. What is going on my dear? Please tell me" Julia said.

"It is nothing Julia. I am suffering from fever" Harold said.

"Did I ever tell you that you are terrible at lying and you have a terrible habit of expressing stress in your face?" Julia said.

Harold couldn't say anything instead. Because Julia was telling the truth. So, he kept looking at her.

Julia said "right now your face is telling me that you are going through something bad. And that bad has turned into worse. Please tell me what it is. And what are you doing standing in front of the window?"

"Nothing I was just" Julia didn't let Harold finish his words. She pushed him away and stood exactly where Harold was standing.

"My God. How did the window glass break?" Julia asked in surprise.

"Someone threw a stone through this window last night" Harold Carter said.

"What? Who? And why?"

"Some young lads may be. I think trying to make fun of me" Harold Carter said.

"Trying to make fun of you? Really Harold? I told you Harold you are a terrible liar darling. No one makes fun of you. Even the young chaps. Anyway, get inside and tell me what is going on" Julia said.

They both went inside and then into Harold's bedroom.

"Take a seat" Julia said.

Harold sat on the chair.

"Now tell me what is going on" Julia Wilson asked in a commanding voice.

Before saying anything to Julia Wilson last night's words from Dorothy came into Harold's mind. "Don't tell her that you are doubting her. Else she will be immensely hurt." Harold waited for a minute before saying anything. Because he needed to come up with an idea which can convince Julia Wilson which is a very hard task.

"Come on. Tell me" Julia said again.

"Oh God, it is very hard to hide anything from you. You are right my love. I am going through a problem. I thought I would solve it myself but now it seems like

I can't. I didn't want to involve you because I thought you might react rudely" Harold said.

"Will you kindly tell me what happened?" Julia asked. She was running out of patience.

"Do you know Paul Collins?" Harold Carter asked.

"Paul Collins? Who is that?" Julia asked in return.

"He is a young member of our library" Harold Carter said.

"So, what happened to him?" Julia asked.

"He was reading 'At the Villa Rose' and he wanted to take the book with him to his home to complete it. Now you know that is strictly prohibited. But that kid was very stubborn. So, Dorothy let him take the book to his home without telling me. She told me that yesterday evening. I know she made a mistake but you know she is a wonderful girl and also Paul is a nice chap. Did you remember I was asking you about that book the day before yesterday?" Harold said.

"Yes, I remember" Julia said.

Harold said "Right. The book was missing because Dorothy gave it to Paul."

"But when? Because I was going through that book the day before yesterday" Julia Wilson said.

"I guess after you left the book on the rack Dorothy gave it to him. But please Julia, don't say anything to either of them. I beg of you" Harold said in a pleading voice.

Julia gave Harold a strange look and then asked—

"Is this really what happened or are you making it up? Because I will ask Dorothy about this. And if she says you were lying, then there will be a huge question about our future Harold. Because I can tell you by looking at your face that you are not telling me the truth. You are hiding something" Julia said.

"You are not believing me? Why should I lie to you?" Harold Carter asked.

"I don't know Harold. You tell me. Because this is not the truth. I know. Are you having an affair Harold?" Julia asked.

"An affair? Really Julia? You are not believing me? After all these years staying together? For the love of God please stop thinking like this. You are the only woman I ever loved. You know that. I am telling the truth. If you don't believe me then ask Dorothy. She will tell you everything" Harold said.

He was trying his best to convince Julia anyhow.

Julia kept quiet for a while and then said—

"I believe you darling. I do. Sorry I doubted you. I won't say anything to Dorothy about this matter but I will tell her to not to do this again".

Harold walked up to her and kissed her on her forehead. Julia kissed him back and said—

"The matter is solved now. So please stop drinking. Eat something and sleep. I will take care of the library."

"Yes, my darling" Harold said and then asked Julia—

"Are you going back to the library?"

"Yes. Why?" Julia asked.

"I think I should go with you. Because the matter is solved now. I can't sleep now Julia. It is 12:10 in the afternoon. I will take another day off" Harold said.

"Alright. Then get dressed quickly. We are getting late. Dorothy is alone there" Julia Wilson said.

"Yes, my love" Harold said and went inside the bathroom.

Julia was relieved. She thought Harold knew everything after listening to Dorothy but now she believes that Harold has no clue about the disappearance of the books. Now she can continue her work with a stress-free mind. No one is here to stop her. This is what she wanted. She never wanted Harold to know about the disappearance of the books. Because that would have created an obstacle to her work.

Harold was a little tense. Because everything he said to Julia is an absolute lie. And Dorothy knows nothing about this. There is a big possibility that she will deny all of this and that's why Harold wants to go to the library today to keep everything normal.

"God have mercy" he said to himself.

When he came out of the bathroom Julia asked him a question which shook him a little bit but somehow, he maintained his confidence.

"Did you bring any booklist from my study room yesterday? I kept it on my study table. It was there till yesterday afternoon. But I couldn't find it in the evening when I went to see it" Julia asked.

"Booklist? I didn't see any booklist in your study table. And what book list are you talking about?" Harold asked.

"It was a list of a few books I wanted to buy. So, I made a list. Well, it must be somewhere else. Don't worry about it. Let's go to work" Julia said.

They both went to the library by Julia's car. Some of the members of the library were standing outside of the main gate and they were talking about something. Something very strange. Julia recognized this by looking at their faces. So she went towards them after getting out of the car and told Harold—

"You go on. I will catch up with you."

"What happened? What's wrong?" Harold Carter asked.

"Nothing. A little curiosity. You go on" Julia said and went towards the group.

Harold took a deep breath and went straight to Dorothy's office. Because he is not going to get any better opportunity again to explain everything to Dorothy. Dorothy was writing something. She was surprised to see Harold.

"Sir? You are here? Is everything alright? Madam Julia came here looking for you. I told her to go to your place. Did she go?" Dorothy asked.

"Yes Dorothy she did. But I have to tell you something" Harold Carter said and explained everything to her.

"Well played Sir. You gave a good reason. Don't feel guilty for making me the culprit. You did the right thing." Dorothy said.

"Yes. But I don't know whether she believed me or not" Harold Carter said in a worried voice.

"Don't worry Sir. She will believe you" Dorothy said.

"Alright Dorothy. Let's get back to work and spend the day like every other day. Because we have to stay normal in front of her. And you were right about the book list. She did find out that it was missing from yesterday. She asked me about it before coming here. But I denied. I didn't have any choice. I can't let her know" Harold Carter said.

"I understand Sir. Be steady. But what will you do?" Dorothy asked.

"I need proof Dorothy. Let's see how I can get it. Anyway, don't worry about this now. Just go to work" Harold Carter said and left Dorothy's office.

It was 5.30 in the evening. The library was about to close down. Harold was standing listlessly at the front gate of the library. It was still a nightmare to him to believe that Julia Wilson is involved behind the disappearance of the books. His heart is telling him that Dorothy is right. Julia is not involved behind all of these. The piece of paper with the disappeared book names is just a coincidence. But his brain was telling him something else. He couldn't listen to his brain and couldn't trust his heart either. All of these thoughts were rushing his mind until he heard sounds of footsteps. He turned around. It was Julia who was coming out of the library. Harold was a little surprised. Because normally Julia leaves the library around 6.30 to 7 in the evening. There is still one hour to go at least.

"Are you leaving now?" Harold Carter asked.

"Yes darling. I have important work" Julia said.

"What work?" Harold Carter asked.

"Flora is suffering from high fever. You remember flora, don't you?" Julia asked.

"Yes, I do remember. Your admirer from the library" Harold Carter said.

"Yes. And I am going to take her to the doctor" Julia said.

"Well, anyone from her family can take her to the doctor. Why you? Come to my place tonight. Let's spend the night together" Harold Carter said and then he kissed Julia Wilson.

Julia Wilson kissed him back but refused Harold's proposal of spending the night together. She said—

"Not tonight darling. I have to take her to the doctor. No one in her family will take the responsibility.

Because if they wanted to, they would have done that by now. She has been suffering from the last two days. I have to take her to the doctor. Another day Harold."

And then she walked towards her car and drove away. For a moment she didn't look back towards Harold. This was enough for Harold. A girl like Julia who loves Harold so much that she never would have refused his proposal. But she did. Dorothy was watching everything from the balcony of the first floor. She came down towards Harold after Julia left.

"What happened Sir? And I didn't know that Madam Julia was leaving this early" Dorothy said.

"She is going to take Flora to the doctor. She has been suffering from high fever from last two days. No one in her family will do the work. So, she is going to do it. She even refused my proposal of spending the night together. She never did that before" Harold said in a melancholy voice.

"Flora? Flora Rogers?" Dorothy asked surprisingly.

"Yes Flora but I don't know her surname. Why?" Harold Carter asked.

"Does she know another person named Flora?" Dorothy asked.

"I don't know Dorothy. Why?" Harold Carter asked.

"If she is talking about Flora Rogers who happens to be a member of our library, was here in the afternoon Sir. And she didn't look unwell. I think Madam Julia must have mentioned someone else" Dorothy said.

Harold was speechless. He couldn't believe his ears. Julia lied on his face. He said—

"God have mercy. When Julia asked me if I remember her, I simply replied "yes I know her and she is a member of our library and Julia said yes."

Dorothy's eyes went big. She said—

"But why did she lie to you? My God, is she really involved?"

"Yes Dorothy. She is involved and she is planning something tonight. Otherwise, she wouldn't have lied. Look Dorothy it doesn't matter how hard it is to believe that Julia is involved, we do have to believe that indeed she is involved and we have to make plans according to that" Harold said.

"Plans? What plans?" Dorothy asked.

"Proof Dorothy. Proof. We need proof. Doesn't matter how. Listen to me. Close the library and go home. I will do the same. I think we both need some time to think about the matter. Think and come up with a plan. I will try to do the same. Come to my house tomorrow evening after library hours and tell me about your thoughts. I will tell you mine" Harold Carter said.

"But what if Madam Julia decides to go with you to your house tomorrow night? Then?" Dorothy asked.

"I will take care of that. Tomorrow's meeting will not change" Harold Carter said.

"Alright Sir" Dorothy said and went inside the library.

Harold went back to his home. As much as tried to think about the matter, he couldn't. He wouldn't be able to see that the police are arresting Julia, the love of his life. He said out loud "enough is enough" and decided to go to the library. Because he knows that Julia is planning something tonight and there is a possibility that she might come to the library. Harold knew tonight will be his only chance to be absolutely sure whether Julia is involved or not before going to the police. Around 11 AM in the night Harold left his house and started walking towards the library. He didn't take his car to avoid detection. It was raining heavily. Harold was wearing a raincoat. Though the library wasn't that far from his house still he decided to walk slowly. He was shivering in the cold. He wanted to see and catch Julia red handed. He was wearing a black suit under the rain coat and his raincoat was also black. A perfect disguise in the night. It took him 25 minutes to reach the library. Harold was very much cautious. Because he knew that Julia wasn't alone.

He stopped 20 to 30 yards before the front gate of the library. The gate was opened. He waited for 2 minutes and then decided to go in. He opened the gate slowly and entered into the front yard of the library. He was about to enter the library when he saw a flash of light. A torch but turned off immediately. It was coming from the second floor. This is the exact floor that Dorothy mentioned yesterday morning. He slowly entered the library. As he was about to go upstairs, he heard a sound of a door being closed. He quickly moved out of the way and hid himself beside a closet full of books. His black dress was helping him to blend into the darkness. It was impossible to find him in the pitch dark although he could see everything.

A woman came down from the second floor. Harold stood still without making any noise. He couldn't believe what he saw. It was Julia Wilson. A torch in one hand and a book in the other hand walked right past him. Though he couldn't see her face, he was absolutely sure that it was Julia. Because she was wearing that dress which was gifted by Harold. He gifted her that dress on her last birthday. She went into her office and Harold stood like a sculpture. He couldn't move. He was standing like a paralysed person. He closed his eyes in horror. A truth he didn't want to face. But then he realised he has to get out of here. All of his senses came back. He quickly went out of the library straight to the footpath and hid himself behind the wall. A few minutes later Julia came out of the main gate. Stood there for a minute. As she was trying to find out whether anyone was following her and then she locked the main gate and left. Harold went down to his knees. He was watching towards Julia's trail as she quietly vanished into the darkness. That's the way to her home. Harold couldn't get up for two to three minutes. But he finally got back on his legs. A drop of tear came down through his chin. He couldn't catch her. He wanted to but he couldn't. How can he? That's the woman he is devoted to. That's the woman he cares and loves more than anybody. He began to walk towards his home with a heavy heart and perhaps the longest walk back to his home.

The Long-Haired Man

England 1950. The lives have begun to settle down after World War II. It was an unstable time for everyone. But life always seems to find its way back to normal. I volunteered for the war. I was a writer by profession. But when the country needed its people the most, that's when I decided to join the armed forces. But I kept on writing even when I was in the army. But my call of duty ended along with the war. As Hitler and Germany faced a defeat in the battle, I put down my guns, kept my uniform in a closet and picked up the pen as my weapon. I saw everything in the war. I experienced it first-hand. The brutality was unbearable for me. One war my entire view point towards the world and its people. So, I started writing anti-war stories and poems. Well, my poems and stories certainly didn't stop the conflict between countries from occurring, but somehow, I believe this from the bottom of my heart that maybe someday somebody will understand the effects of conflict and maybe that day my poems and stories will make an impact in their hearts. So now I am determined that I will spend my time writing novels and poems against the war. I used to live in London. But after the war I needed a quiet place, away from all the chaos. And after a long search for a peaceful place, I finally decided to move to Wiveliscombe, a little town in Somerset.

I fell in love with the place the moment I shifted there. The neighbourhood was peaceful and friendly. It didn't take me a long time to settle in there. I got a wonderful home for a very low price. Wiveliscombe also has a small library but it was enough for me to write my novels. So, my life was going exactly to the direction where I expected it to go till, I met a person who eventually became my brother and whose brotherhood changed the entire direction of my life from where it was going. My time with him till now has given me the best part of my life. The memories and stories I gathered are undeniably by far the best I could ever have. After watching deaths and blood for more than two and a half years, I needed a fresh start and this man gave me exactly what I wanted. He is my neighbour. He lives beside my house. But my first impression of him was a little weird due to a lot of reasons. He had an unusual look. Well, he still has the same look but it is unusual nevertheless. Long hair, which almost reached the middle of the spinal cord, was indeed unusual for a man in the 1950's. Because then, men used to do a rather different type of fashion particularly to the hair.

He was nearly six feet tall and was very slim in figure and a musician by profession, a guitarist. He had, well he still has an obsession about Blues music, a genre originated in the deep south of the United States. I used to listen to his Bluesy music every evening from seven o'clock to nine o'clock. Well, I still listen to his Bluesy music but the timing has changed since we stay in the same house now. My friendship started with him in a rather unusual way, or to be honest, in a sad way. An incident which took place two weeks after I shifted to Somerset was the beginning of a brotherhood and a friendship. This is how it all started.

"Good morning, Mr Bennett" Willie Brooks said.

Willie Brooks. A young chap who stays two houses after my house. A very enthusiastic person and very much interested in football. He was the first person I spoke to after coming to Wiveliscombe and since then he became a friend of mine. But he was immensely interested in someone and very soon I also grew interest in the same person and to be honest, my interest grew a step further.

"Good morning, Willie. Come, join me for a cup of tea" I said.

"Oh, certainly Mr Bennett, I still have ten minutes. Are you enjoying your stay here?" Willie asked.

"Yes. This is exactly what I wanted. Far from all the chaos" I said with a smile of relief on my face.

"Well if you are trying to escape from the chaos then you might have come to the right place but chaos is not physical all the time. Sometimes it is mental. And if you watch closely, you can find chaos here too. The only difference is you can't see it. It is invisible. It is in the mind of people" Willie said.

"You seem to know a lot about chaos, aren't you? But this is not a chaotic place. I have been here since past two weeks and I didn't find any chaos" I said.

Willie smiled and said "have you heard about Miss Evelyn Foster?"

I said "Yes, I did. Everyone says she is very beautiful. But I haven't had the chance to see her yet."

"She is not just beautiful Mr Bennett. She is the most beautiful woman in the entire world" Willie said.

Willie's words surprised me a bit. Clearly, he has a weakness for her.

I said "In the entire world? So you are one of her loyal admirers? Aren't you Willie?"

"You wouldn't say that Mr Bennett if you would have seen her. But it's bad luck that she is about to be married to a man who is not worthy of her. Not worthy at all. I don't know how she even chose him to be her future husband" Willie said these words with anguish.

"So, you have feelings for her, don't you?" I asked.

Willie said "certainly not. All I want is her happiness. Anyway, I have to go now. Goodbye Mr Bennett."

Willie stood up and went through the opened door of my garden and immediately he came back running again and said "there she is. Come outside, have a look at her Mr Bennet."

"Who?" I asked.

"Evelyn, Mr Bennett, who else. See for yourself" Willie said.

So I went outside to see the most beautiful woman in the world. Willie was breathing heavily. And I can understand why. Just like every man in Wiveliscombe, Willie loves her and wants to marry her too. And Miss Evelyn Foster was coming closer to us. Willie's face started to become red. Indeed, she was beautiful. Though I am not married, I always admired beauty. She looked at me with a lot of curiosity.

"Good morning, Evelyn. This is Mr Richard Bennett. He came here two weeks ago" Willie said in a hurry.

Thank God, he said it. Because I don't think I could have. I was consumed by her beauty. I thought I was watching her, but soon I realized that I was staring at her when Willie looked at me awkwardly. And I had to take my eyes off.

"Oh, you are the war hero from London? I heard about you" she said in her mild voice.

I said "Definitely I am from London but certainly not a war hero. I did what my country needed me to do."

"It is your modesty Mr Bennett. We all know how tough it was for our soldiers. So, every person who fought in the war is a war hero. You protected our country by putting your life in danger. We will always be in your debt" Evelyn said.

Well, this was it. After a long time, somebody praised what I did in the war. I was already consumed by her beauty and to add to that, her words were enough to nail the coffin. Just like Willie, I too got attracted to her. I couldn't say anything in response to her words. Willie was watching me and smiling. Maybe he was telling me silently "I told you Mr Bennett. She is the most beautiful woman in the world." Perhaps Evelyn understood my situation. So, she said—

"Alright gentlemen, see you later. And Mr Bennett, be a little careful of your neighbour. He is a little mad."

"Who is a little mad? Should I be afraid?" I asked curiously.

Evelyn said "You haven't seen that weird man yet? The long-haired musician?"

I said "I saw him once from my window. But I listen to his guitar tunes every day. He seems like a good guitarist."

Evelyn laughed and started walking where she was going. Both I and Willie were looking at her as she was going away.

Willie said "do you believe me now? I told you she is the most beautiful woman in this world. Anyway, have a nice day Sir." Willie left.

I stood there for a few more minutes before I went back inside the house. For the first time in my life, I was thinking of writing a poem of love. By far I had stayed away from this world of love and romance. But after watching a beauty like Evelyn, it was very hard to get rid of the temptation of entering into the world of love. But why does everyone think that my neighbour is mad? Because the way he looks? Of course, he is a bit weird but I never thought he was mad. But I couldn't think about my long-haired neighbour for a very long time because Evelyn was unsettling my mind again and again. Her beauty was mesmerising. I spent the entire day thinking of Evelyn. She doesn't know I am a writer. So, I decided to surprise her with a romantic poem. I didn't go to the library that day. After a long thought, I finally came up with a poem which I thought was enough to impress her. It was not a proper romantic poem but the affection was there. Around eight o'clock in the night I saw her again crossing my house. I kept looking at her until she went out of my sight. My heart was beating faster. I couldn't sleep that night. I woke up early the next morning and stood at the front gate of my garden hoping to meet her again. It was 8.30 in the morning. Evelyn's house is not so far from my house. Every morning around eight o clock she goes to the church and comes back around 8.45. She crosses my house on her way back from the church every day. Normally I don't stay more than eight o clock in my garden. I finish my breakfast within that time period and stay busy with my writing and then around ten in the morning I go to the library. Yesterday was exceptional. Willie came around exactly when I was about to get inside the house. So, we spoke in the garden and that's why I was able to meet Evelyn. I wanted to make today another exceptional day but my luck didn't favour me. Whether she didn't go to the church or she came back early. I was standing there hopeless only then I heard a heavy voice telling me "Are you alright?"

I looked up and saw my neighbour. That long hair again.

Seeming I was feeling little weird he said with a smile on his face—

"I suppose you are a little surprised by my look like everyone else here? Well, you might have already heard that the people of Wiveliscombe call me a mad man. But I can assure you Mr Bennett you have nothing to fear from me. I am a modest man and just like you I too like to avoid chaos."

Being a little awkward I quickly said "I don't listen to the people. And moreover, I am a huge admirer of your music. The tunes you play are indeed praiseworthy."

"Thank you, Mr Bennett. At least someone likes my music" he replied with joy.

I said "Well, I don't think there has ever been any question about your music. The only concern they have is the way you look. You do know this long hair of yours is a little strange right?"

He said "Yes, I know. But I like it this way. And by the way how is your writing going? I would like to read your anti-war stories and poems."

I was taken by surprise. No one in Wiveliscombe knows that I am a writer. Because I haven't told anyone about this. All they know is I am a war veteran.

"How do you know I am a writer?" I asked him.

He said nothing in reply. Just said "never mind" and went inside his home.

I was messed up in my head. Didn't have a clue what was going on. Not only does he know that I am a writer but he also knows my subject of writing. Anti-war poems and stories. How in the earth is this possible? The more I was thinking about his words, the more confused I became. So, I let all that go away from my mind. Because what I hoped didn't happen. I went inside the house to get ready for the library. The rest of the day was uneventful. I walked intentionally slow my way to the library and my way back to the house in the hope of meeting Evelyn for once. But that didn't happen either. I came back home that evening feeling downhearted. I even carried the poem which I wrote for her to the library with me hoping if by any chance I see her, I will give it to her. I was very much upset. I read the poem for one last time before tearing it up in agony and threw it out of the window. I was feeling heart broken and I needed to refresh myself. I was thinking what to do and right then I heard the sweet sound of guitar. My neighbour has started playing again. If anything can refresh me right now, it is music. And because I spoke to him this morning, the hesitation was also gone. And not only that, his guitar playing also reminded me of his strange words he said to me this morning. So, I decided to go to his house. He was still playing guitar when I left my home. And as I was about to knock on the front door he shouted from upstairs—

"Door's open Mr Bennett. Come upstairs."

I was taken by surprise again. Is he some sort of magician or what? How could he possibly know it was me? I literally ran upstairs. He was writing music in his manuscript.

"Welcome Mr Bennett. Please take a seat" he told me pointing towards a chair.

"Are you a magician?" I asked him.

"Certainly not Mr Bennett. You know I am a musician" he said without even looking at me.

"Then how did you know that it was me who was standing at your doorstep? And not only that, you also know that I am a writer and I write anti-war poem" I said those last few words, almost shouting.

"Please calm down Mr Bennett. I can see you have become very much excited about what I told you this morning. Would you like a cup of coffee?" he asked rather politely.

I felt a bit ashamed of my behaviour. "Forgive me Mr…… Oh Jesus. I didn't even ask your name" I closed my eyes in shame.

"I know you are heart broken right now. People do behave like this in this type of circumstances. This is normal. I would have done the same. So don't be ashamed. And my name is Wilfred Dankworth" he said.

"Ah! Mr Dankworth, you are right. My mind is all over the place. Yes, I will take a cup of coffee."

"There you go" he handed me a cup of coffee and took one for himself.

"Alright please solve these mysteries which have been eating me up, one since this morning and another when you told me to come upstairs."

"These are not mysteries, Mr Bennett. This is a simple observation" Wilfred said with a smile.

"Please explain this to me, Wilfred. I can call you Wilfred, right? Because you seem to be my age" I said.

"Of course, you can. Alright, which one do you want to know first?" Wilfred asked.

"Start with the later one. How did you know I was coming to your house?" I asked.

He said—

"Alright. Listen very carefully. You came here to live a peaceful happy life, far away from all the chaos. That's why you avoid gatherings. You like to stay alone and undisturbed. You spend almost half of the day in the library reading books and you come back to your house every evening around 7.30PM. This routine of yours continues to happen till you met Evelyn Foster. Yesterday you met her for the first time and I can say that for sure, because you were looking at her like you had never seen her before. Watching a beauty for the first time puts a different look on the face of a person rather than watching a beauty for the second time. The first time it is just astonishment. But in the second time it is the urge of watching that beauty again. This morning you had that urge in your face. You were standing at the main gate of your garden to meet her again just like yesterday. But she didn't show up. So you were disappointed and heartbroken. And that's why I asked you, are you alright? Because I saw you and Willie spoke to her yesterday. I still remember that look on your face. Then you spent the whole of yesterday in your house which you hadn't done before. Moreover, this morning you were waiting for her, instead I surprised you by saying that you are a writer and you write anti-war stories and poems. You were surprised. Then today you left for the library wearing a wonderful dress with a rose in the pocket of your coat. I never saw you dressed like this, especially putting rose on your coat on your way to the library. So, you dressed like this to impress her. But just like this morning, you didn't meet her. And you also came early from the library today. As I said earlier, you normally come back from the library around 7.30 PM. But today you came around 6.45 PM. Because right now it is 7.30 PM. So two things were eating your mind up. One is the utter disappointment of not seeing Evelyn and the second is the words I said to you this morning. When things like this happen, we normally try to find something which will distract us. Now, some people try to get distracted by speaking to someone else. But you don't like to do that. And right after you came back home, I started playing the guitar. The wonderful sounds of strings. Now what can be better than music to cheer up a person's mind? We all know that nothing can distract a person and give a calm and peaceful mind more than music. Then I saw you leaving your house. Now you told me this morning that you are a big admirer of my playing style. So, it is easy to guess that you were coming to my house. Because you wanted to get distracted and also you wanted the answer about 'how did I know about you'? And if you can remember, I stopped playing when you were standing at my doorstep, because I saw you leaving and I knew you are coming to my house. That's why I stopped playing. Though I didn't see you coming. All I heard was the sound of footsteps. And as you know that no one visits my place, because they think I am mad, then who else could it have been except you? So, it wasn't a hard guess that the person coming to my house is you."

I couldn't speak for at least 2 minutes which I thought was 10 minutes. He took me to an entirely different world. It took me sometimes to come back to reality. Because I never seen anyone explaining something with this much accuracy without even watching the entire incident.

I asked him "you guessed all of these?"

"This is not a guess Richard. This is called observation or also you can call it detection. After detecting the facts, I came to a conclusion which is known as deduction. So, you detect something and then deduct that based on the facts" Wilfred said.

Watching that startled look on my face he said "I am also a consultant detective."

"A detective? But you are a musician by profession, right?" I asked.

"I am a musician and a consultant detective" Wilfred said.

"Just like Sherlock Holmes?" I asked.

He smiled and said "Sherlock is a million time better than me my friend. I am nothing to him. Even I am nothing to the great Hercule Poirot and not even Father Brown."

"Alright, now based on your detection tell me how did you know that I am a writer?" I asked.

Wilfred said—

"Mainly for two reasons. One, since you have arrived here, I saw you brought a bunch of loose papers in a brown packet, twice in two weeks. Now who needs that much loose paper unless the person is a writer? A normal person who doesn't write that much will never require a bunch of loose papers."

"That was straight forward. And the second one?" I asked.

He said "Well, the second one is by luck. Have you noticed that drop of ink on your right thumb?"

I looked at my right thumb and said "of course I did. My pen is leaking ink."

"Right. Now do you know when the ink leaks from a pen?" he asked.

I said "yes. When you use that pen for a longer duration. My god." I looked at Wilfred.

He was smiling and nodding his head.

"No one uses a pen for a longer duration unless he or she is a writer" I said with pride.

"So? Wasn't that hard, was it? And another proof that you are a writer is, if you would have used that pen for a longer duration but only once in a day, that drop of ink on your right thumb would have faded away. But it didn't. That means you not only use that pen for a longer duration but also quite often in a day. And that's why that drop of ink on your right thumb stays intact" Wilfred said.

"But how did you know that I write anti-war poems?" I asked.

He said—

"You are a war veteran who came to Wiveliscombe for peace. Now if that person is a writer, isn't it obvious that he will write anti-war stories and poems? Poems which stand for peace?"

"It sounds like bread and butter when you explain this. I never could have thought like that" I said.

"But before I listen to your anti-war poems, I am very much eager to listen to that poem you wrote for Evelyn" Wilfred a said with a naughty smile on his face.

Though my eyes widened for a moment but immediately controlling that expression I said "I didn't write anything for her."

"Of course, you wrote. You wanted to impress her today but not just by your dress. When a person wants to impress a woman, he will try to impress her by doing something he does best. If I want to impress a woman, I will compose romantic music for her. Because that's what I do best. And in your case my friend, it has to be a romantic poem. Well, it can't be a love letter. Because the matter didn't reach that far I suppose. Or did it?" Wilfred asked. There was a hint of mockery in his words.

"Alright, you are taunting me now" I said.

"Then tell me the poem" Wilfred said.

"I tore it up when I came back home" I said.

"But you do remember it, don't you? How can you forget something you wrote for a person whose beauty consumed you? So, don't be hesitant Richard. There is no shame telling me a romantic poem" Wilfred said.

"Alright listen

"Who are you?" asked the Lord of light.

"I have come in behalf of my Queen,

I am a Knight from the north, which has gone dark again,

But her reign is yet to be defined."

"I swear an oath to protect her with my life,

And here I stand with my sword.

I bow before you the Lord of light,

Give me power and the Lion's roar."

"She is the rightful Queen, first of her name,

Who has never been crowned before.

She is the Queen of mercy, she is the Queen of love,

Who took a vow, to serve the poor."

"So, we stand together, as we stood before,

Fighting against all the odds.

We will storm the battle, we will win the hearts,

With the blessings of all the Gods.""

"It is from the medieval period, isn't it? It sounds like that. And by the way, though it doesn't sound like a proper romantic poem to me, it is indeed wonderful. Well, this poem is the proof of your affection for Evelyn. But my friend, listen to me. Evelyn is not for you. I know Willie told you that she is marrying someone who is not worthy of her. Believe me Richard, that's all rubbish. James is a very good man. I know this from the bottom of my heart. The only reason Willie hates James is because he is jealous. And not only has he, almost half of the Wiveliscombe hates James because of the same reason. They are happy with each other. And I think she is a little young for you. Isn't she?" Wilfred asked.

I finally laughed and said "Yes, I understood that. I am not thinking about her anymore."

"Good. Since your broken heart has come back to whole again, how about I play a new tune for you?" Wilfred said with joy and I welcomed him.

That evening was one of the most pleasant evenings I spent in the last five years. We ate dinner together at Wilfred's home. He insisted.

He said "since this day is the first day of our friendship, why shouldn't we celebrate this over a wonderful dinner?"

We talked about a lot of things after dinner. I didn't know that he had a library in his house. And as much I was talking to him, I began to realize that our lives are exactly the same. We both need each other. And that evening brought us together. I asked him a weird question while leaving his house—

"Wilfred, will you make me your assistant in the upcoming cases of yours?"

"You already are my dear Watson" Wilfred said with a lot of happiness.

Two Deaths and a Detective

"So how many cases have you solved yet?" I asked.

I was sitting in Wilfred's library. It was a Sunday morning. He has such a good collection of books and some of the rare ones. I was flipping the pages of a music theory book. Wilfred was writing musical notes in his manuscript. Without looking at me he said—

"Four cases. I know an officer in Scotland Yard. His name is Raymond Wright. I met him during a case in London. Back then I used to teach music in Trinity College. Unwillingly I got involved in a case and eventually solved it. He loved the way solved the case. Since then, he came to me so many times regarding different cases and I told him the solution. But I don't consider those cases as my own. Because I hardly worked there. I only consider those cases where a client directly came to me with a problem or the police directly wants involvement. There are only two such cases."

I was about to ask him another question, just then I heard a knock on the front door. Wilfred went to open the door. A minute later he came back with a police personal.

"Speak of the devil and he shall appear. I was telling him how I met you" Wilfred said pointing towards me.

Then he introduced the two of us—

"This is Richard Bennett. My new friend and neighbour. He is a war veteran and a writer by profession. And Richard, this Raymond Wright. The bright future of Scotland Yard."

"Again Wilfred? Stop bragging about me. Your mocking will never end right? And Mr Bennett, it is nice to meet you. You must be a nice person. Because this man usually doesn't make friendship with anyone. Well, I would like to see your work one day. Anyway, let me tell you why I have come here in the early morning. Around 6 AM this morning, a fisherman found a dead body near the river Tone. He informed the Somerset police. We got the news two hours later. According to Somerset police, that man is not from here. You know this is not a big city like London. So, most of the people know each other. Some of them did see the body but none of them identified the man. The Somerset police couldn't understand how he died. It is a possible murder. But there is also a possibility of natural death too. But it looks like a murder. The man is well dressed. Now the question is why would someone like him go to the river side in the middle of the night? That's why I think it is a murder. I would have come a little earlier, but was stuck in some written work. I told Somerset police to keep the body there. I believe no one here knows that you are a detective. Well, this will come out now" Raymond said.

"That's alright Raymond. Give us 10 minutes my friend. Let's get dressed. Because we can't go to a crime scene wearing night dresses" Wilfred said.

"Us? Is he coming?" Raymond pointed towards me.

"Oh, I forgot to tell you Raymond. Richard is my Watson or also you can call him Hastings. From now on He will assist me in every case" Wilfred said.

"Well, just like Arthur Conan Doyle, he is a big admirer of Agatha Christie. Whenever she publishes a book on Hercule Poirot, Wilfred Dankworth will be among those people to buy the book first. I once told him you are just like Poirot and Holmes but he disagreed with me" Raymond said.

I said "Well I told him the same thing last night. But he didn't agree with me either."

"You can continue this conversation with Raymond on our way to the crime scene, Richard. Please get dressed as early as possible. We are getting late" Wilfred shouted from his bedroom.

Twenty minutes later I, Wilfred and Raymond got into Raymond's car and drove off to the place where the body was found. By the time we reached there, the place was crowded by local people. The body was found inside a bush near the river. A constable walked towards us.

Pointing to Wilfred, Raymond said "This man is a consultant detective and actively works with Scotland Yard. He will help in our investigation."

"No problem, Sir. He found the body" the constable pointed towards an old man who looked still in shock.

"You can ask him questions if you want" the constable said.

"That will not be necessary. He is still shaking. Let him be. Though it is less possible but did he see anyone in the area when he discovered the body? Anyone" Wilfred asked.

The constable said "No Sir. There was no one. At least he didn't see anybody. He was walking around the river side. That's when he found the body."

"Alright. Let me inspect the body."

We walked towards the dead man. He was well dressed. Near six feet tall. He was wearing a black suit and brown shoes. Both looked a bit costly. Wilfred sat beside the body. He was looking at the dead man without a blink. Then he rolled up the sleeves of the dead man's coat and said—

"He came from London, most probably."

"London? How can you say that?" Raymond asked.

"Look at under his sleeves. The name of the tailor is there. H. Huntsman and sons. This tailor shop is only found in London. He can be from Manchester or Birmingham. But there is a higher possibility that he came from London. His face seems a little familiar to me. I think I saw him before" Wilfred said.

"Where?" Raymond asked.

"That's what I can't remember now. Anyway, how long ago did he die?" Wilfred asked.

"According to the doctor he died between 12.30 AM to 1.30 AM in the night" Raymond said.

"What is this?" Wilfred took his face almost closed to the dead man's neck.

"What?" we both asked.

"Come, take a look" Wilfred said.

"Dear god. It looks like a needle had been pushed through his neck. Was he poisoned?" Raymond asked.

"There is a possibility of poisoning him but I don't think he was poisoned. Otherwise, there would have been some changes in the skin colour, because he died almost eight to ten hours ago. Well, no doubt it is a murder. But not by poison. I think he was attacked by a group of people who injected him with a sedative and then suffocated him to death. He was killed somewhere else, probably in London and then was carried over here, probably by a car" Wilfred said.

"How can you say that?" I asked.

Wilfred said—

"Well, the police have already confirmed that he is not from here. So, if he came here himself, he came whether by car or by train. Now the police have already searched the whole Wiveliscombe but they didn't find any car. So, all that is left is, he came by train. Raymond, call the station master here. If this man came by train, then the station master might have seen him. And if you remember, it was raining till this morning today. And the man died around 1.30 AM. It was still raining heavily and this whole area was full of mud. Now look under our shoes. It is full of mud as well as the sides of the shoes. But look at his shoes. It's still shining. And not a sign of mud under the shoe or beside. So, he didn't come walking to the river side. He was brought here dead and threw off. Call the station master. His words can be vital".

A constable went to the Taunton railway station for the station master. Wilfred was still concerned.

"Still can't remember where you saw him?" I asked.

Wilfred nodded his head in disappointment.

The station master came half an hour later. He trembled a bit after seeing the dead body and said with a shaken voice "My goodness me. Is he dead?"

"Yes Sir. Now, can you tell me have you seen this man before? Well, before you answer, I must tell you that he most probably came from London, whether yesterday or a day before yesterday. Now, have you seen him during your time of duty?" Wilfred asked.

The station master took a good look at the dead man and then said "no Sir. I would remember if I had seen him. I am sure."

Raymond said "Thank you very much Sir. You may leave. Well, it looks like you are right again Wilfred. He was brought here by car after he was murdered. But I don't understand one thing. Why would someone take the hassle to carry a dead body from London to Somerset? They could have left the body anywhere in London or from wherever he came from."

Wilfred said "Just to be on the safer side and delaying the investigation, I guess. If you remove a dead body to a place where that person is unknown, then it will take some time to identify that person's identity. That will give the criminals a window of opportunity to escape or remove every possible evidence. We have to go to London. My hunch is telling me he is from London."

"Mr Bennett, a letter came from the library. You weren't home, so the postman gave the letter to me. I came here because I thought you would be here" I turned around hearing this familiar voice. It was Willie.

"Library! Goodness me. Now I remember where I saw him" Wilfred almost shouted in excitement.

"Where?" I asked in most curiosity.

Wilfred said "I read an interview about him in the newspaper. Still can't remember his name but I am pretty sure I still have that newspaper in my house. Come with me both of you. And Willie, stay here. If anyone asks for us, take him or her to my house. It is very important you stay here."

Before Willie could have asked us anything we left the place in hurry. Raymond almost flew his car. We covered the twenty minutes road within ten minutes. All three of us rushed into Wilfred's library room. He keeps his old newspapers there.

"The interview came in the newspaper last month. Check for any interview by a librarian" Wilfred said.

So, without wasting any time all three of us started looking.

"There it is. I got it. Take a look. It is the same person" Wilfred said.

We almost jumped on the newspaper.

"Well done my friend. You reduced half of our work" Raymond tapped on Wilfred's back.

I was still looking at the newspaper.

Wilfred said "his name is Harold Carter. He is the owner and the chief librarian of J.C Library. His father James Carter built that Library. I met Harold Carter once when I used to stay in London but it was a long time ago. That's why it went out of my head."

"But Wilfred, why would someone murder a librarian?" I asked.

"That's what we have to find out. Alright Raymond, take the boy to London. Inform the J.C Library. You take your car with you. We will come by train" Wilfred said.

Raymond was about to leave, right then Willie came with a constable.

"I have a news Sir" said the constable to Raymond.

"I got a telephone call from London. A woman named Dorothy came to Scotland Yard to report a missing person. Name of that person is Harold Carter. He is the chief librarian of J.C library. The woman said he is missing from last night. She went to his home today morning. But he wasn't there. The inspector said Harold Carter's description is matching with the dead man we found here."

"We already found that out" Raymond said and handed over the newspaper to the constable.

"Oh, I see," said the constable.

"Sent a telegram to Scotland Yard saying we are coming back. Don't tell anything about Harold Carter's death and tell the woman to wait there" Raymond said.

Willie was listening to our conversation in amazement.

"How did you two get involved in this mess?" He asked me and Wilfred.

I said "You misunderstood this man, Willie. Perhaps the entire Wiveliscombe misunderstood him. For your kind information, Wilfred Dankworth is not only a musician but also a consultant detective who works with Scotland Yard. Maybe he looks a little weird but he is very much humble compared to his knowledge in music, detection and deduction. Anyway, we are going to London to investigate this case. As you are my good friend, I have a request for you. May I?"

"Of course, Mr Bennett" Willie said.

"Can you keep a watch on our houses till we get back from London, once a day perhaps?" I asked.

"I will Mr Bennett. Don't worry about it. And Mr Dankworth, I beg a pardon for my judgment on you" Willie said.

"That's all right Willie. And thank you for watching our houses."

Around 2 PM in the afternoon we took a train from Taunton railway station towards Paddington London. It takes around two and a half hours to reach Paddington from Taunton railway station. Raymond left early with the dead body. Wilfred was very quiet on the train. So, I started to read the newspaper but couldn't concentrate. One question was troubling me. Wilfred was looking out of the window but somehow, he understood the state of my mind. He said—

"You are still thinking about that question, aren't you?"

"Seriously Wilfred? You didn't even look at me. Yes, the same question. I mean why would someone kill a librarian?" I asked.

Wilfred said "for so many reasons. Maybe he saw something that he shouldn't have seen or something fishy is going on in his library, illegal perhaps. I guess he might have found out what was going on. Or maybe he himself was involved behind something illegal and perhaps betrayed his group. That's why his mouth was shut forever."

We reached Scotland Yard around 5.30 PM. Raymond reached before us. He has already done all the necessary arrangements. From there we went to the library. A woman was waiting at the front gate with an anxious face. As soon as we arrived there, she came towards us with a lot of questions.

"Did you find him? I am getting worried."

"Dorothy, right?" Wilfred asked.

"Yes Sir" Dorothy said. "Let's go to your home Dorothy. I assume you are in charge of the library in Mr Carter's absence?" Wilfred asked.

"Yes Sir" Dorothy said.

"Tell someone to take care of the library for today. Tell them you are feeling sick and going home. We have a lot to discuss" Wilfred said.

Dorothy's apartment is 15 minutes from the library. She lives alone there. She is unmarried.

"Tell me Sir what's going on" she said immediately after entering her apartment.

Wilfred said "I suppose I brought bad news for you Dorothy. Around six in the morning today, a fisherman found a dead body of a person near the river Tone in Wiveliscombe, who unfortunately happened to be Harold Carter. He was murdered, Dorothy."

"No. This can't be possible" Dorothy broke into tears.

I couldn't look at her. After 15 minutes she recovered herself a bit but still she was sobbing. I gave her a glass of water but she didn't drink it.

"I told him not to pursue this alone. But he didn't listen to me" she said.

"What not to pursue Dorothy? Tell us everything you know" Wilfred said.

Dorothy said "Sir, a weird thing is happening in the library. The books are disappearing, I don't know how. But then after a few days they are also coming back themselves."

"Books are disappearing themselves? How in the earth is that possible?" I asked.

"That's what I don't know Sir. Mr Carter found out himself. I didn't. He told me about the disappearance of the books. At first, I didn't believe him. I thought maybe the books were misplaced and kept somewhere else or maybe the books were taken or stolen. But he wasn't ready to believe me. Because it was impossible to snatch a book from the library Sir. We have guards who check every member of the library when they come out. The guards never found any proof. So, I told him some worker must have misplaced the books. But then I didn't find the books myself after at least five days. They were missing somehow. But then unbelievably all those books which had gone missing came back themselves. So, I also began to doubt that something was wrong. Two days ago, I came to the library after midnight to check what was going on. I didn't tell Mr Carter about this. He was with Madam Julia that night in his house."

"Who is Julia Wilson?"

Dorothy paused for a few seconds at Wilfred's question and then said—

"Madam Julia is Mr Carter's lover. She also works in this library. Their relationship is a little complicated. They know each other and love each other from the last six years but for some reason Madam Julia never agrees to marry him. They were meeting after a while. He was very happy. So, I didn't tell him that I am going to check what's happening in the library. I reached the library around 12.30 AM and I saw a glimpse of light turned on and immediately turned off at the second floor. I went inside the gate for a closer look and I saw a torch light moving around the bookshelves. The next morning, I told Mr Carter everything I saw. He was very angry with me. He told me he will check himself and then report to the police. That day Madam Julia didn't come to the library. So, Mr Carter went to see her and said he will be back in an hour. Then around 4 PM, Paul Collins, one of the members of our library, told me that Mr Carter met him at the front gate and told him that he is feeling sick and he is going home. I will close the library and will go to his house. He has something to tell me. So, I went to his house after closing the library.

He was fully drunk and looked devastated. I asked him what happened. Instead of answering my question he gave me two pieces of paper. One was a threat letter Sir. It said 'Stay of out of whatever is happening in the library. Don't try to contact the police. Else you will be dead.' And the other paper contained the name of those books which disappeared from the library. He found the threat letter in the back seat of his car when he came back from Madam Julia's house and the paper which contained the name of all those books which had disappeared from Madam Julia's house. The hand writing of that list was Madam Julia's Sir. We both were sure about this. This is where he started to believe that Madam Julia is involved in this matter. And when I was about to leave Mr Carter's house, I heard a sound of breaking glass. So, I went to check and saw a paper wrapped in a stone. It was thrown from outside through the window. It was another letter Sir. The handwriting was the same as the first letter. It said 'Stop doing your own investigation. I will not harm you unless you do something silly. And don't inform the police. Else there will be consequences.' I told him not to go alone and he said he won't. He took the next day off but then in the afternoon he came to the library with Madam Julia. I was a little surprised to see him. He always had a problem expressing his feelings through his face.

Madam Julia doubted that maybe there is something wrong with Mr Carter. So, the next day before coming to the library she went to Mr Carter's house and asked him directly. Mr Carter did well. He came up with a brilliant idea to convince Madam Julia. He said that one of the young members of our library, Paul Collins, wanted to take a book home to complete the story. Now because of some circumstances borrowing books from the library is prohibited. Mr Carter said to Madam Julia that I allowed Paul to take the book home and that's why he was tense. Because he was afraid if Madam Julia got to know about this, she might fire me. That's why instead of taking the day off, he came to the library to inform me about what he said to Madam Julia. Though Madam Julia never asked me about the matter.

We spent the rest of the day normally. Then around 5.30 PM in the evening I saw Mr Carter talking to Madam Julia in front of the main gate. After Madam Julia drove away, I went to Mr Carter. Again, he was looking dishearten. I asked him what happened. In reply what he said made me speechless. He was asking Madam Julia to spend the night with him. But Madam Julia refused his proposal by saying that she has to take Flora, one of our members, to the doctor because she has been suffering from fever for the last two days. And no one in her family will take her to the doctor. But unfortunately, Sir Madam Julia was lying. Flora was present in the library that didn't look unwell at all. Flora is a regular member of our library. She comes every day in the morning around 10.30 A.M. Though Mr Carter remembered her name but forgot how she looked. He was very upset because Madam Julia lied to him and also very much sure that she is involved in the disappearance of the books. He was continuously saying I need proof Dorothy. Then he told me to go home and think about how to get proof against Madam Julia. He said he will do the same. I was about to meet him in his house tonight to tell him about my thoughts.

I told him the day before yesterday to not go to the library alone in the night. That will be too risky. Watching him yesterday evening I thought he was able to control him. But I had no idea that he would take such a drastic step and would go to the library alone."

"Does Julia Wilson know about Harold Carter's disappearance? Did she come to the library today?" Wilfred asked.

"No Sir. She didn't come today. And I didn't go to her place. I don't think she knows. Is Madam Julia involved in Mr Carter's death?" Dorothy asked.

"It will not be right to say that she is involved without any proof" Wilfred said.

"But who wrote these letters? Mr Carter doubted that she was alone. She may be working with some other people" Dorothy said.

"Right now, it is not possible to say who wrote those letters. But those threat letters and a list of book names are not enough to convict Julia Wilson of Harold Carter's murder. Anyway, what happened to your right ear?" Wilfred Dorothy asked.

I was a little astounded by that question and so was Raymond.

"My right ear?" Dorothy was taken by surprise.

"Yes" Wilfred said.

Dorothy said "A little accident Sir."

"How did that happen?" Wilfred asked.

"I fell down from the stairs Sir and my ear got smashed into the wall" Dorothy said.

"I guess that happened recently, right? Because your ear is still bleeding. Go see a doctor first and then go to the library and tell everyone about Mr Carter's death" Wilfred said.

"I am alright Sir. I can go to the library now" Dorothy said.

"No Dorothy. You need to see a doctor. Do what I am telling you" Wilfred said with a little authority.

"Where will you go now?" Dorothy asked.

"Miss Julia Wilson's house. She needs to know. Anyway, do you have those threat letters and the book list?" Wilfred asked.

"I have the threat letters Sir" Dorothy said.

"Give them to me and go see a doctor" Wilfred said.

Dorothy handed him the threat letters and we came out of her house.

Julia Wilson's house was a bit far from Dorothy's house. It took almost half an hour to reach her house. Although the house wasn't anything special, overall, it was good. She has a garage and a car of her own. I and Raymond were looking at the house. Wilfred knocked on the door. Once, twice and thrice but no one answered. So, we called her name but still no answer.

I said "maybe she is not home."

But Wilfred was concerned.

He said "If she is not home, then why is the garbage still in the dustbin? She would definitely have cleaned it before she was leaving, wouldn't she? But she didn't. That means she is still inside the house and yet she didn't open the door."

"Maybe she is sleeping. Dorothy said she was unwell yesterday" I said.

"Sleeping? Now? No Richard. I am getting a hunch that something is wrong. Let's break the door" Wilfred said.

We broke the door with five pushes. Wilfred was the first person to get in. I looked at the dustbin. Really there was a lot of garbage. Raymond came last. Julia Wilson's drawing room was nifty and clean. She has her own bookshelves filled with different types of books. I was fascinated by her collection. I couldn't believe the fact that someone who has a very rich taste in books can be involved in criminal activities.

Wilfred said "She is not here. Let's check her bedroom."

Three of us went inside the bedroom together and were stunned by silence. My heart almost stopped biting. I think both Wilfred and Raymond felt the same way. Julia Wilson was lying on her bed with no life inside her body. Her eyes were open. Her mouth was open. Her left hand was hanging from the edge of the bed. The colour of her face already turned a little yellow.

"Good Lord. I didn't expect that" Raymond said.

"Neither did I" Wilfred said.

I was speechless. It was a bolt from the blue.

"Wilfred, suicide letter" Raymond handed a letter to Wilfred.

Wilfred read out loud—

"I killed Harold. He was creating problems in my business. He was asking too many questions. He even told Dorothy about the disappearance of the books. I tried to keep him out of this. I even threatened him with two letters but he didn't listen to me. So he left me with no choice but to kill him. I never wanted to do this. But now I can't sleep. He was the only person who cared about me and I killed him. I can't stay here alone. I am going to meet him now. Bury my body beside him. I hope he forgives me, Julia"

"So, Harold Carter was right. Indeed, Julia Wilson was involved. It is an open and shut case then. But where is the poison?" Raymond asked and went to search for it in the kitchen.

I was already looking for it. "There it is. Cyanide. Do you think she…" I turned towards Wilfred to ask him something but I stopped. He was staring at Miss Wilson's left hand which was hanging from the edge of the bed. Then he took her wrist in his palm and began to check the fingers and then kept it as it was. Then he lay down on the floor on his chest and started to look under the furniture. Then he stretched his right hand under the furniture and reached for something. Everything looked very mysterious to me. I couldn't resist of asking—

"What is it you looking for?"

He said "Nothing. Just a little curiosity."

Then after a few seconds he stood back up. I didn't know whether he got what he was looking for or not but I couldn't ask any question. His face was very serious. By the time Raymond came in the room empty handed and said—

"The poison is not in the kitchen. Ah, you already got it." I gave him the bottle.

He said "Well, Wilfred It is an open and shut case. Everything is clear as water by this suicide note."

But for some reason Wilfred wasn't getting convinced.

He was looking inside the drawers of Miss Wilson's study table. He was down on his one knee. After a few minutes he stood up with a piece of paper. There was something written on it—

"Room number 12. Second floor. Third rack etc."

Wilfred was looking at those writings with a lot of attention. He was looking a little confused.

I asked "What is this, Wilfred? Who wrote this?"

But Wilfred didn't answer.

I asked "what is bothering you?"

He said "Nothing. Richard, you stay here for a minute. I am coming back. Raymond, come with me."

He took Raymond with him to the drawing room. I couldn't hear what they were talking about except once

Raymond said loudly "what? Are you sure about this?" I couldn't hear what Wilfred said in return. He came back after ten minutes or so and said—

"Richard, try to find out anything with Miss Wilson's handwriting on it. Anything. You search in the drawing and study room. I am searching the bedroom."

So, I went to search the drawing room first and then the study room. I searched every drawer and even the books. Because sometimes people write their names on the front page of the book. But unbelievably I didn't find anything which contains Julia Wilson's handwriting. So, I went to tell this to Wilfred. And he didn't find anything either.

"Nothing?" he asked.

I said "No."

"Not even in the books?" he asked.

"No. Not even in a single book" I said.

"But how in the earth is this possible? There is not a single piece of paper in the house which contains Julia Wilson's handwriting. Have you ever seen this before Richard? At least there has to be the documents. Even those are not here. Alright, let me see the books" Wilfred said.

We both went to the study room. Wilfred started to check the books and suddenly said "My God."

"What?" I asked.

"Nothing. Richard, Raymond is still outside ordering his constables. Ask him to come here" he said.

I went outside and came back with Raymond.

"Yes Wilfred?" Raymond asked.

"I need a car. I will take Julia Wilson's books with me in Wiveliscombe today. It is very important. I will come back tomorrow. Richard will come with me. Tell somebody to pack all of these books in the car. By that time, let's go to Harold Carter's house."

I was taken by surprise.

I said "The case is solved, right? Because Raymond said it is an open and shut case. And I also can see that. Then what will you do with the books?"

"Ah, Richard. Now I want to tell you just like Sherlock tells Watson. It is not that simple my dear Watson. I can assure you that. Take this newspaper and let's go."

He handed me the Daily Herald.

I asked "what will I do with this?"

"Just keep this with you. We will need this later."

We came outside. By then the doctor reached the place. He went inside to examine the body. The police had already announced Julia Wilson's death to the neighbourhood. A lot of curious people gathered in front of Miss Wilson's house. All of them had a lot of questions in their eyes. I looked at Wilfred to ask "what now" but I stopped. He was looking at an old man. The old man was standing there and listening to the police with very much attention. At first, he didn't notice that we were looking at him but the moment he found out that we were watching him, he started to leave.

"Who is that, Wilfred?" I asked.

"Someone with a lot of interest in Miss Wilson's death perhaps" Wilfred said.

"How do you know that?" I asked.

"He gave me signs unknowingly. We need to talk to him. You wait here Richard. I have something to ask Raymond" Wilfred said and walked towards Raymond.

I tried to think of what Wilfred saw. I was also watching that old man. I didn't see anything significant in particular. Wilfred was talking to Raymond. Then he went towards Julia Wilson's garage. The garage was closed. Wilfred asked a constable to open the garage. A constable went inside the house and came back a few minutes later with a key. He opened the door of the garage. Wilfred went inside. The garage wasn't too big. I could see a car inside covered by a big cloth. Wilfred was watching the car suspiciously. I didn't understand what he was watching. He stood there for about five minutes and then came back to me.

He said "An Ambulance is coming. Miss Wilson's body will be sent to the morgue."

The doctor came outside. Raymond asked—

"Well doctor, time of death?"

"In between 1 AM to 3 AM" the doctor said.

"She was poisoned right?" Wilfred asked.

"Yes" the doctor said went towards his car.

Wilfred was shaking his head. Something was unsettling him from inside.

"Is there anything wrong Wilfred?" I asked.

"What do you think" Wilfred asked me instead of answering my question.

"I think there is something wrong. Because in a normal viewpoint this is indeed an open and shut case. Julia Wilson killed Mr Harold Carter and then committed suicide. It is clearly visible but still you are not convinced. Maybe I can't detect the way you do but even a child can say that there are a lot of questions in your eyes. It is clear that Miss Julia Wilson committed suicide but still for some reason you were watching her left hand suspiciously. I did notice that. You searched her entire house to find her hand writing. Then you drew a piece of paper from her study table's drawer and watched that with a lot of questions. Then we came outside and you were looking at that old man. When I asked you about him, you said he could be somebody with a lot of interest in Miss Wilson's death. That means he has something to do with Miss Wilson's Suicide. Then you were observing, yes, this is the word I will use. You were literally observing Miss Wilson's car suspiciously. I mean if it is just a suicide, then there is no need to do all of this right? Why are you doubting Wilfred? Because your activities are saying something is not right. What's wrong Wilfred?" I asked.

"So, you noticed. Well done, Richard. But I can't say anything now unless I understand. For now, just bear with me. Anyway, we need to go to Harold Carter's house. We also need to talk to Flora Rogers. We will go to Mr Carter's house first and then Flora's house" Wilfred said.

By the time we left Miss Wilson's house Raymond sent her body to the morgue and told some of his officers to inform the library about the incident. One officer already started packing the books when we left Chiswell Street. Raymond said he will be there till all the books are packed and ready. Wilfred told Raymond to bring the car to Flora's house. From there we will go to Wiveliscombe. It took a while to reach Mr Carter's house because his house is a bit far from Chiswell Street. We didn't have the key to the main door of his house. But it wasn't necessary. Because the door wasn't locked. So, we opened the door and entered inside the house. And the moment I entered his house, I stumbled on something that fell down on the floor. Wilfred went a little ahead of me. He heard the sound of my body hitting the floor. He came charging in.

"My goodness. Are you alright? What happened?" he asked.

I said "Look at this place? Looks like a storm passed through. The whole place is messed up. Who did this?"

"Moriarty" Wilfred said and laughed.

"Come on Wilfred. This is not the time to joke. I just fell down" I said in anger.

"Calm down my friend. This is the work of those people who killed Mr Carter. Come inside the bedroom" Wilfred said and went towards the bedroom.

"Hold on a minute. What did you just say?" I was surprised to hear what Wilfred said.

"What did I say?" Wilfred asked.

"I thought Miss Wilson killed Mr Carter" I said.

"That's correct" Wilfred said.

"But you just said this is the work of those people who killed Harold Carter. People?" I asked.

"You saw Harold Carter's body didn't you Richard?" Wilfred asked.

"Of course, I did. I am not blind" I said.

"Right. You also saw Miss Wilson's body" Wilfred said.

"Yes, I did" I said.

"Right. Now tell me Richard, was it possible for Miss Wilson to kill a healthy and quite strong person like Harold Carter alone?" Wilfred asked.

My eyes widened. Wilfred is right. It was not possible for Miss Wilson to Mr Carter unless there was help.

"Now you understand?" Wilfred asked.

"Yes. But how many were there?" I asked.

"Time will tell that. But for now, come inside" Wilfred said.

I went after him.

"Look at the flowers. They have fallen on the ground. Now take a look at these broken glasses. Most probably these broken glasses are from another flower Vase. The flowers were in the Vass before. Do you remember I told you and Raymond this morning that Harold was killed here in London? Well, he was killed right here, inside his house, in this very room. I think at first, they tried to knock him out cold but Harold Carter resisted. As you know he was a strong person. So, he put up a fight. I think he reached for this Vass to use it as a weapon but he couldn't. When they couldn't knock him out, they used the sedative to make him unconscious and then suffocated him to death" Wilfred stopped.

"But why is the room messed up? All the clothes, papers are all over the place. Why do this?" I asked.

"Because they were searching for something here what we were searching in Miss Julia Wilson's house a while ago."

"A sample of her handwriting?" I asked.

"Yes, my friend" Wilfred said.

"But why? Why is suddenly her handwriting become so important?"

"I will explain everything to you Richard. But first we have to find a sample of Miss Wilson's handwriting" Wilfred said.

After searching the entire house finally, I found a sample of Julia Wilson's handwriting. That book list Dorothy was talking about. It was inside the pocket of one of Mr Carter's coats.

"I guess they didn't care to look inside the pocket" I said.

"Maybe they were in hurry. Because they had a body to move far away from here. And then they had another thing to do" Wilfred said.

"What?" I asked.

He said "as I said Richard, I will explain everything to you. But please don't ask any more questions."

Raymond came 15 minutes later. Wilfred explained everything to Raymond.

He said "they made a very cleaver plan but every criminal always leaves a clue behind. Anyway, everything has been arranged."

"What arranged?" I asked.

Raymond said "I put some guards in the front yard and back yard of the library if by chance anything goes wrong. But Wilfred, please tell me what will you do with these books?"

"There is something I have to check. I will explain once I come back" Wilfred said.

"Alright. Comeback as early as possible" Raymond said.

"Yes. But before we have to talk to flora" Wilfred said.

The Painter

We didn't have Flora's address. So, we had to go to the library to get it. Flora's house is in Brabant Court. It is not so far from J.C Library. It took 15 minutes to reach Flora's house by car. She lives in the ground floor of a five-storey apartment. The door was locked. We knocked on the door. A few minutes later a girl opened door and looked at us with inquisitive look and asked—

"May I help you gentlemen?"

"Are you Miss Flora Rogers?" Raymond asked.

"Yes. But who are you people?" asked Flora.

Raymond said "My name is Raymond Wright. I am from Scotland Yard. This is Wilfred Dankworth. A consultant detective and this is Richard Bennett, our friend."

Flora looked at us for a while and then said "How can I help you inspector?"

It felt like she decided what to say in those few minutes.

"Can we come in? I have to tell you something very important" Raymond said.

We went inside her apartment. Her apartment was full of paintings. Different types of paintings. She also has her own bookshelf just like Miss Wilson's. Wilfred did notice her paintings. He was watching them with a lot of attention. I saw a glimpse of appreciation on his face though he didn't express any of that. He went towards her bookshelf.

"Did you hear anything from the library?" Raymond asked.

"What?" Flora asked.

And right at that moment Wilfred looked at her. I don't know why. Raymond didn't notice but I did. There was a surprise in his eyes. I couldn't figure out why he was surprised to hear the word 'what'. But then immediately he moved his attention towards those books and began to watch them again.

"I have a bad news, Flora. Mr Harold Carter and Miss Julia Wilson are dead. Probably last night" Raymond said.

Flora was stunned listening to this. She almost screamed and said—

"Mr Carter? Oh my God. How did this happen? And also, Julia? This is not possible. I spoke to her last evening. She was absolutely fine. And I also saw Mr Carter at the library yesterday. How in the earth is this possible?

"But this is what happened, Flora. I am so sorry" Raymond said.

Oh my dear Julia. She was a very good friend of mine. How did they die?" Flora asked.

She was trying very hard to control her emotion but she could hold herself for long and finally she broke into tears. Raymond tried to calm her down. Finally, Flora managed herself and then said—

"They both were at the finest of their health. Please tell me how they died?" she asked again.

"Mr Harold Carter was murdered by Julia Wilson. We found Mr Carter's body in Wiveliscombe which is far away from here. After killing Mr Carter Miss Wilson took his body there and dumped him. Then she came back home and couldn't believe the fact that she killed the person she loved. So, in guilt she committed suicide and left a suicide note. After finding out about Mr Carter and Miss Wilson's relationship, we went to her house and there we found her dead. She poisoned herself" Raymond said.

"But this is impossible. Julia can't kill Mr Carter and neither would she commit suicide. They were in love for a long time. I don't believe you" Flora said.

"It doesn't matter how bitter it sounds Flora but that is the truth" Raymond said.

"Why didn't you go to the library today? You go to the library everyday right Flora? Around 10.30 A.M. Dorothy told us. Why didn't you go today?" Wilfred asked.

Flora was a little surprised by this question. She stared at Wilfred for a minute and then said—

"I wasn't feeling well. That's why I didn't go to the library."

"You are suffering from fever I guess, just the way you were suffering yesterday?" Wilfred asked.

"Yesterday? I was alright yesterday. And I am not suffering from fever. It is a little headache" Flora said.

Wilfred looked at her and then smiled.

"Are you not believing me?" asked Flora in anger.

But Wilfred didn't answer her question. Instead, he said—

"I will need something from you if you have."

"What?" Flora asked.

"A piece of paper. Just wait a while" Wilfred said. And then turned towards Raymond and said—

"You proceed with everything I told you Raymond. I will take care of this. Just told your driver to bring the car here. We will go to Wiveliscombe directly from here."

"Alright" Raymond said and left.

Wilfred sat on a couch and said—

"Seat down Flora. We need to talk."

Flora sat on a chair at the opposite side of Wilfred.

"Did you know that a strange incident was happening in the library? Tell me the truth Flora. I know you do. It will be better for everyone if you tell me the truth." Wilfred said.

Flora was looking towards the floor. She kept looking there for a while and then slowly looked at Wilfred and then she nodded her head.

Wilfred said "So you knew about the disappearance of the books? Who told you? Julia Wilson, I suppose?"

Flora nodded her head again.

"Did you know that Mr Carter was doubting Miss Wilson? He thought Miss Wilson was the one who was stealing the books for some reason. And Mr Carter also doubted that she wasn't alone. She had company. Did you know about this?" Wilfred asked.

"What? Mr Carter knew? He doubted Julia? How could he? And why?" asked Flora

"A day before yesterday Mr Carter went to Miss Wilson's house to see her. There he found a piece of paper. That paper contained the names of those books which had disappeared from the library. The handwriting was Miss Wilson's. And not only that, he also got two threat letters that same day because he noticed what was happening in the library and started asking questions. That is when he started to doubt Miss Wilson. So he began to investigate the matter on his own. Because of those threat letters and the piece of paper he found in Miss Wilson's house, he thought Julia Wilson was stealing the books" Wilfred said.

"But that's not the truth Sir. Julia wasn't stealing. In fact, she was the first person to discover that the books were disappearing. She kept Mr Carter out of this because she knew whatever was happening was not legal. So, it is not possible that Julia killed Mr Carter. You are making a mistake Mr Dankworth" Flora said.

"Alright Flora. I believe you. Now tell me everything you know" Wilfred said.

"I joined the J.C Library five months ago and Julia was the first person I spoke to. We became friends very soon and started to go to each other's houses. A few months ago, she told a peculiar thing to me. She told me some of the books disappeared for a few days and then suddenly came back. At first, I didn't believe her because this is not possible. I thought she was joking. But she kept telling me about this every day that the books are going and coming back mysteriously.

So, I said, alright show me how. One day she took me to the second floor in room number 21 and told me to remember the names of all the books. I went to that room so many times before. So, I knew the names of all those books. It was not hard for me to remember. Only two books were taken by two of the readers that day. Then three days later Julia told me that one book is missing. I checked myself Sir. She was right. Indeed, one book was missing. Because I went to check this after all the readers left the library. Julia was with me. You may not know that our library doesn't allow their readers to lend books to home. And they have guards outside who check everyone at the time of entry and also at the time of exit. Even Julia, Mr Carter and Dorothy. This system was started by Mr Carter's father which Mr Carter was continuing. So where did that book go?

Now according to Julia someone was stealing the books for some purpose. So, it is impossible to steal inside the library hours. Julia believed it was happening in or after midnight. She didn't do any of this Sir. She was the one who tried to stop this. Julia was one of the most honest women I have ever seen in my life. So, someone else had done it and definitely not inside the library hours. They must have done this by the night. Julia was about to tell the matter to Mr Carter but she was waiting for proof. She wanted to see how the books were disappearing. So, she used to go to the library at midnight very often. Because she used to believe that midnight is the best time to do things like this. But she didn't find anything and the disappearance of the books kept going on.

I told her to tell Mr Carter about the matter. But I don't know why she was hesitating. Then a few days ago she told me that she thinks that Mr Carter knows about the disappearance of the books. But then yesterday, around afternoon she came to the library. She was not supposed to come yesterday. I was standing outside and was talking to some of the members of the library. She came and took me to her office and said that she went to Mr Carter's house today. She talked to him. But he knows nothing. She was very relieved. Because she didn't want to involve him in this matter without any proof. Then she told me that she will go to the library last night. I also wanted to go but she said no. She wanted to go alone. I don't know whether she went last night or not. And now you are telling me that she killed Mr Carter and then committed suicide. This is not possible Sir. Julia was killed just like Harold Carter." Flora said.

"So according to you Julia Wilson didn't commit suicide?" Wilfred asked.

"Yes Sir" Flora said.

"Why do you think that?" Wilfred asked.

"Because whatever is happening in the library is illegal Sir and Julia wanted to stop this. So, it is obvious that whoever is doing this didn't take Julia's action so kindly. Julia was causing problems. So, they killed her. And now you are telling me that Mr Carter also knew about the matter. So, they killed Mr Carter too" Flora said.

"But Flora each and every proof is indicating that Miss Julia Wilson did commit suicide. We found a bottle of cyanide from her house. Now is it possible that somebody will force her to take poison? I don't think so. Do you?" Wilfred asked.

"Definitely not. And I also don't know what proofs are indicating but I know these from the bottom of my heart that Julia didn't kill Mr Carter and didn't commit suicide. She loved him very much. But I don't understand why you are throwing away the chance of Julia being murdered. There is a huge possibility that she could be killed. Because she found out about the disappearance of those books" Flora almost screamed.

"Even if we believe your words for a moment that indeed Miss Julia Wilson was killed, who do you think killed her? Do you doubt anyone?" Wilfred asked.

"How can I say that? I have no idea who is behind this. All I know is they found out that both Julia and Mr Carter were investigating the matter. So, they killed her and also Mr Carter" Flora said.

Wilfred smiled and said—

"Did Miss Julia Wilson doubt anyone? Did she ever mention any name to you?"

"No Sir. She didn't tell me any names. And even if she doubted anyone, she never told me" Flora said.

"Alright Flora, I will show you two things now. You will understand why I am saying Miss Julia Wilson killed Mr Carter" Wilfred said and then he took out a piece of paper from a pocket of his coat and handed that over to me and told me to read out loud.

It was a letter. It said—

"Julia, I never ever thought you could do this to me. I loved you from the bottom of my heart. I gave you everything you ever needed and wanted from me and yet you betrayed me. You thought I didn't notice what was going on in the library. But you were wrong Julia. I knew everything but I never thought you are the one behind all this. When I went to your house two days ago, I saw a piece of paper on your desk containing the names of those books which had disappeared and came back mysteriously. It was your handwriting, Julia.

On that same day I got two threat letters because I was sticking my nose into the matter and started investigating on my own. Even yesterday evening when I asked you to come with me to my home, you lied to me saying that you need to take Flora to the doctor. You said she was suffering from fever. You knew that I don't remember Flora's face. So, you took the chance. But the matter of fact is Flora was present on that day and wasn't ill at all. But even after all of these, I still didn't believe that you are involved in this matter. But now I am. I saw you tonight, Julia. I went to the library tonight to find out whether you are really involved or not. I saw you coming down from the second floor. You were wearing the dress I gifted you. I know you didn't expect me there. Otherwise, you wouldn't have taken the chance to wear it. What were you doing there in the middle of the night? Stealing another book? I know you are not doing this alone. Maybe you have been pressurised by someone. Because I know you can't do this to me. Please tell me who is forcing you to do this? There is still a way out, Julia. It is still not late. Don't talk to me about this. Maybe they are watching and listening. Write to me. Let me help you. Harold."

Flora's eyes widened. She said—

"But this letter doesn't prove that Julia killed Mr Carter. Julia went to the library in the middle of the night to catch the thief. Mr Carter had made a mistake. May he saw Julia but she wasn't stealing books."

"Yes. You are right, flora. Indeed, this letter doesn't prove that Miss Julia Wilson killed Mr Carter. But this will" Wilfred said and took out a torn piece of a dress perhaps and asked flora—

"Do you recognize this? Look carefully."

Flora took the torn piece of clothing in her hand. I could see that her hands were shaking. Her expression changed in a blink of an eye. She asked trembling voice—

"Where did you get this?"

"In Harold Carter's house. When we went to Mr Carter house the place was a mess. I believe when the killer tried to kill Mr Carter, he gave the killer a fight. I think there was more than one person. I found this in Mr Carter's house and by your expression I can understand that this torn piece of cloth is from Miss Wilson's dress which was gifted to her by Mr Carter. I think when Miss Wilson tried to kill him, he grabbed her dress in defence and as a result this part of her dress was torn out" Wilfred said.

Flora broke into tears once again and was continuously saying—

"No, no, no, no, no. This is not possible."

Wilfred was watching Flora. Once she stopped crying Wilfred asked—

"But did you tell me everything Flora?"

"Yes, I did" Flora said.

"No, you didn't. You are still hiding something" Wilfred said.

"What will I hide? And why should I hide?" Flora asked.

Wilfred didn't say anything. Then he stood up and went towards a painting. It was kept in the canvas. I saw this when we came inside her apartment.

"Did you paint this?" Wilfred asked.

"Yes" Flora replied.

"This is India, right?" Wilfred asked.

"Yes Sir" Flora said.

"Have you ever been to India or is it a creation of your imagination?" Wilfred asked.

"I never been to India, Sir. My parents went there four years ago. They travelled the entire country and told me several stories of India. The picture you are watching is a result of that. My parents told me stories. I imagined them and painted that imagination into canvas" Flora said.

"This is your signature, right?" Wilfred asked.

"Yes Sir" Flora said.

Flora used to do signatures in her paintings.

"You are a wonderful girl, Flora. It would have been better if you would have told me everything. Anyway, take care of yourself" Wilfred said.

"You said you need a piece of paper from me" Flora said.

"Not anymore" Wilfred replied.

"Can I ask you a question Sir?" Flora asked.

We were about to leave. Both of us turned around. Flora said—

"This is not an open and shut case isn't it Sir? Because if it was then you wouldn't have been asking questions. And the police would have shut the case by now. It is not that simple, isn't it?"

Wilfred looked at Flora and gave her a smile. We came out of her house.

The car was waiting for us outside of Flora's house. One police constable was standing beside the car. Wilfred told him to wait there. There was a sign of frown in Wilfred's eyes. For some reason he was feeling uncomfortable.

"What's wrong?" I asked.

"Did you see Miss Wilson's car before leaving her house?" Wilfred asked.

"Yes, I did" I said.

"Did you find anything strange about it?" he asked again.

I thought for a while and said—

"No. I don't remember anything in particular. Why? Did you spot something?"

"It was raining throughout last night, do you remember? In fact, when we reached London, it was raining then too" Wilfred said.

"So what? What does this have to do with her car?" I asked.

"Her car wasn't wet, Richard. And neither her car's tires were dirty" Wilfred said.

I looked at Wilfred. His eyes were sparkling. I asked—

"What are you trying to say?"

Wilfred said "The distance between Miss Wilson's house and the library is not that close. It takes approximately forty-five minutes to reach the library from her house. Maybe a little more or less but nevertheless it is not possible to go there without a car. So, if she would have used her car to go to the library, that car should have been wet and there should have been dirt on the tires. Just think about this Richard, how long she was outside of her home. More than eight hours at least. Like I said, it was raining heavily throughout last night. She might have gone out between 11.30 to 12. She went to the library. Waited for Mr Carter to come. Then she followed him to his home with or without her car. Went inside Mr Carter's house. Killed him. Then took his body and drove a near three- and half-hour road from London to Wiveliscombe. Dumbed his body. Drove again three and a half hours back to London to her house and then committed suicide. And during this entire time her car was wetting in the rain. We found the car covered by a big piece of cloth in her garage but neither the cloth nor the car was wet. How in the earth is that possible?"

"My God. So, you are saying" I stopped in the middle.

"You are right Richard. That car never left the garage. And not only are that, also the timing of the two deaths not matching if Miss Wilson is the killer." Wilfred said.

"That means?" I asked.

"That means lots of doubt Richard. Lots of doubt. Anyway, let's go home. We have a huge task ahead of us and we have to finish this tonight." Wilfred said.

Two Alphabets

It was evening when we reached Wiveliscombe.

I said "Wilfred, I kept quiet for a long time. Now you have to tell me what's going on. You said Miss Wilson committed suicide but you keep asking questions. You brought all of Miss Wilson's book here in Wiveliscombe. Why?"

"Alright. I will. But first we have to put these books in my library" Wilfred said.

We kept all the books in Wilfred's library within 10 minutes.

"Alright Richard, ask me what do you want to know." Wilfred said.

"Did Julia Wilson commit suicide or not? And did she kill Harold Carter? Because your strange behaviour telling me something else" I said.

"By far it looks like this. But there are so many questions which haven't been answered yet" Wilfred said.

"What questions?" I asked.

"Flora Rogers. She lied about two things" Wilfred said.

"What?" I asked.

"She was the first person to know about Julia Wilson's death. But she didn't tell us that" Wilfred said.

My eyes have become widened.

"What are you saying? Flora knew? But how?" I asked.

"By this newspaper" and handed me the Daily Herald and then asked—

"Do you remember this? I gave this to you while leaving Miss Wilson's house."

I nodded my head and said "Yes. I do remember. But how does this newspaper prove that Flora was the first person to know about Miss Wilson's death?"

"Ah Richard. You didn't notice, did you? You should have. Because you searched Miss Wilson's drawing room and that's where she used to keep all the newspapers" Wilfred said.

I said "of course I saw. But what that has to do with Flora's knowledge of Miss Wilson's death?"

"Detection my dear Richard. Indeed, you saw those newspapers but missed one little detail" Wilfred said.

"What detail?" I asked.

"Do you remember the name of those bunch of newspapers?" Wilfred asked.

I tried to remember but I couldn't. The matter of fact is indeed I didn't notice the name of the newspaper.

"Like I said you didn't notice. Anyway, Miss Julia Wilson used to read The Times. Not The Herald" Wilfred said.

"So what?" I asked.

"A person who reads The Times, why all of a sudden, he/she will buy The Herald? An entirely different newspaper? In fact, in the entire house there was not a single Herald except this one. Now if you can remember in Flora's drawing room, where we were seating with her, there was a bunch of newspaper on a table beside the couch where she was seating on. Do you remember?" Wilfred asked.

"Yes. I do. Goodness gracious me. Those were The Herald" I said with astonishment.

"Yes, my dear Richard. Those newspapers were The Herald. Flora kept some of the truth hidden from me. I know she used to go to the library in the night with Miss Julia Wilson. Miss Wilson didn't go alone. Remember what Flora said? She said she only knew that Miss Wilson goes to the library in the middle of the night. She was lying. Not only she knew but she used to go with her. Well, I am telling this because I have proof. Now if for a moment we believe that Miss Wilson killed Harold Carter and the master mind behind the disappearance of the books, then she went to the library last night. But for some reason Flora didn't go with her and that's why she came to her house this morning to ask her about last night. I think the front door was open when she reached Miss Wilson's house. She went inside the house and found Miss Wilson dead. Now you can understand what happened to her that time. Perhaps she was frozen but eventually she realised that she has to leave immediately. Because if anyone finds her with Miss Wilson's body she would be in trouble. But this is where her nerves worked out. Even in this terrible circumstances she was able to open the windows beside the front door. Then she came out of the house. Locked the door from inside by reaching the door lock through the window from outside and kept the window close and left the place. But during all these hastes she dropped the newspaper inside Miss Wilson's bed room. Neither you nor Raymond saw this. But I did and that's when I picked it up."

"But why someone will commit suicide by keeping the front door open? So that it becomes easy to find her body? No Wilfred I can't quiet digest this. And In fact, I never heard about this type of incident before" I said.

"Me too Richard and that's where all those questions come which haven't been answered yet. Miss Wilson went to library last night but her car didn't get wet. And not only that, she was wearing a different dress when we found her dead. But the torn piece of cloths I found in Mr Carer's house was from a different dress. And unbelievably that dress is missing from her house."

Wilfred stopped. I was looking at him with disbelief. It was this easy. I could never think like this. I guess Wilfred understood what I was thinking. He smiled at me and said—

"Everything becomes easy when you notice it my friend."

"But why Flora lied to us?" I asked.

"I think she was scared. She thought we may will doubt her and can put her name into the suspect list. For now, this is the only explanation" Wilfred said.

"Alright. Now tell me why did you bring all Miss Wilson's books?"

"I will. But tell me this do you know what we were trying to find in Miss Wilson's house?" Wilfred asked.

"Of course, I do. We were trying to find any document or anything which has Julia Wilson's handwriting on it" I said.

"Right. But unfortunately, we found nothing. Doesn't it look peculiar to you? Because this is quite astonishing that a person who works in a library doesn't have any paper containing her hand writing. How in the world is this possible?" Wilfred said.

"What are you trying to say?" I asked.

Wilfred looked at me and said—

"There were some papers in her house which did have her handwriting on them but somebody or some people removed those papers from there."

"Some people? I didn't quite understand" I said.

"Richard, I believe Miss Wilson didn't committed suicide. She was murdered" Wilfred said in a very stoned voice.

"Murdered?" I almost stood up from the chair. "But that suicide note?" I asked.

Wilfred said "she didn't write it. Someone else wrote it by copying her handwriting."

"But why?" I asked.

He said "to make it look like a suicide."

"But Miss Wilson was involved in the disappearances of the books, right?" I asked.

"No my friend. She was not involved. She was framed. The killer played Harold Carter against her own lover because he was asking questions."

"But the threat letters? That piece of paper containing all the name of the books which had disappeared? And also, that letter which Mr Carter wrote himself after coming back from the library that he has seen Julia Wilson there" I asked.

"Those threat letters were not written by Miss Wilson. But take a closer look at these two papers" Wilfred said and gave me two pieces of paper. One was the paper containing all the names of the disappeared books. And the second one was suicide note.

"Now take a look at the handwriting of these two letters. Do you see any difference?" Wilfred asked.

"They look similar to me" I said.

"Look carefully Richard" Wilfred said.

So almost put my face inside those papers.

"Do you find any difference?" he asked again.

"The handwriting of this paper which contains the name of those books is close to that handwriting of the suicide note but they are not exact. There are some differences. My God. Are you saying that two different people wrote this?" I asked.

"Right. That's my point. The handwriting used to write book names was Miss Julia Wilson's real handwriting. Think about it Richard. This book list was made way before the threat letters and the rest. Because she was investigating on her own and she had no idea that Mr Carter knew the about the disappearances of the books. That's why she kept that book list openly on the table because no one to doubt. So, this handwriting is Miss Julia Wilson's real handwriting. But the suicide note was not written by her. Now take a look at these two threat letters and the suicide note. These two letters were written by the same person" Wilfred handed me those two threat letters.

"Where did you get it?" I asked.

"Where did I get it? Dorothy gave this to me in front of you. Now you need a doctor Richard because you have started to forget things. Are you sure you didn't leave the army with any head injury?" Wilfred said.

I looked at Wilfred in anger. He laughed and said—

"Alright. Now take a closer look."

"Yes, they are written by the same person. The handwriting is similar" I said.

"Right. Now pick the alphabet "i" and "p" from those two threat letters and match them with the "i" and "p" written in the suicide note. Aren't they identical?" Wilfred asked.

"Goodness gracious me. They look absolute similar" I said in lots of excitement.

"Right. Now have you ever seen that someone who is about to commit suicide, wrote a suicide note in different handwriting? Because that is impossible to do. Miss Wilson was about to take her life. There is not a single possibility that she would have been in that frame of mind to change her handwriting and then write the suicide note." Wilfred said.

Now things started to be little clear.

I said "No. I never saw anything like this before. You are right. It is not possible for anyone. Because that person will not be in that state of mind to change handwriting at the time of suicide. This has to be written by someone else."

"And if you look carefully that is not a suicide note. That's almost a confession. She had just killed her lover a while ago. And now she wants to take her own life because of guilt. But unbelievably she was still in that state of mind to write all these things. How is this possible? Yes, people do write confession in suicide letters to let the world know why she or he is taking that step but those are different circumstances and this was entirely different circumstances. Because if Miss Wilson was involved, then she knew the risks. It was just a matter of time that Mr Carter finds out what was going on in the library. So, the chances of eliminating him was always there because when you do an illegal business, you don't really care about your loved ones, do you? Because at that point money becomes bigger than human lives" Wilfred said.

I nodded my head in consent and asked—

"Then who wrote this threat letters and the suicide note?"

"Undoubtedly one of the killers. And not only that. Do you remember what I said about the timing of their deaths? The timing of the two deaths is not matching with the incident. Mr Carter was murdered in between 1 to 3 AM. Miss Wilson was murdered in between 2 to 5 AM. Even if we think that Miss Wilson killed Mr Carter, in that case like I said before she left her house around 11.30 or 12 AM. She travelled that entire distance by food in a rainy night. A distance which takes forty-five minutes to cover by car. If she went by foot, it would have taken at least one and a half hour to reach the library. So, if she had left at 11.30, then she would have reached the around 1 AM. Then she killed Mr Carter and carried the dead body to Wiveliscombe and dumped it there. But the question is how did she travel this far? By foot? And even if we think that Miss Wilson used one of her associate's car instead of her because her car wasn't wet, still the timing is not matching. Going to the library, killing Mr Carter, dumping his body in Wiveliscombe, then coming back to London will take near about eight hours. How did they manage the entire process within four hours?"

Because both Julia Wilson and Harold Carter died in between 1 to 5 AM. How is this possible? Wilfred said.

I said "Maybe they had two cars. May be there was three people and all of them have cars. One car took the Mr Carter's body to Wiveliscombe and another car dropped Julia Wilson in her house."

"And then that person killed her? One of her associates? Don't forget Miss Wilson didn't commit suicide. Then why would her associate will kill her?" Wilfred asked.

I said "For money. If they remove Julia Wilson from the equation then everything will be theirs."

"You are forgetting one thing Richard. The key to enter inside the library in the middle of the night was that person who works inside the library or at least somehow found a way to get inside. If Julia Wilson was that person, then killing her won't help the other two. No Richard. She was not behind this. I believe she died because she came close to the truth. Perhaps she knew the person behind this" Wilfred said.

"Now tell me how Julia Wilson was killed? If she herself didn't take the poison, then who poisoned her?" I asked.

Wilfred said "I do have a theory but that's my imagination. But one thing is sure. Miss Julia Wilson knew the killers. She let them in. Like I said before there was more than one person and they were there to kill her with that poison. And there is one more reason why I am saying this is a murder. There was a stain of blood on in the floor underneath the bed. Although the blood stain was almost dried when I found it. Raymond didn't see it and neither did you. If someone is dying of poison, then why there would be blood on the floor?"

"Is that Miss Wilson's blood?" I asked.

"No. That is not possible. She was killed by cyanide. It is not possible there will be blood on the floor" Wilfred said.

"Then that blood stain was on the floor could be of the killers?" I asked.

"Absolutely. According to me Miss Wilson resisted when they were trying to poison her and somehow, she was able to hurt one of the killers" Wilfred said.

I said "I think I am slowly getting what had happened. The killers put the threat letter in Harold Carter's car when he was in Julia Wilson's house. The paper which contains the names of the disappeared books was unknown them by that time. They didn't know about this. And I think they still don't know about this. Because that book list was with Mr Carter the entire time. Because I found that from one of his coat's pockets. All they knew that Harold Carter was asking questions. So, they threatened him. But he didn't stop. Instead, he was making plans with Dorothy to investigate the matter. This could have made a significant tension in the mind of the killers. So, they gave Mr Carter the second threat letter. But still he refused to stop. So, they killed him. Right?"

"Well done, Hastings. Yes. I believe this is exactly what happened. And one more thing is there which proves that Julia Wilson wasn't involved" Wilfred said.

"What?" I asked.

Wilfred said "Suppose we both work in a library and you are involved in something illegal. Now I am doubting that something is wrong but I don't know what is wrong and who is behind this. So, I started asking questions. But I am still not sure what is going on. Now that shouldn't bother you as long as you are hidden in the shadows. But still if you want to take steps, will you be that stupid to write a threat letter to me which will certainly make me believe that indeed there is something going on? Because if you do so, then you are intentionally letting me know that you are involved. I don't think Miss Julia Wilson was that much stupid. Although Mr Carter was doubting her, but he still didn't have any proof except one book list. So, sending him a threat letter to let him know that there is a problem is absolutely rubbish. No Richard. Miss Wilson was not that stupid."

Wilfred was absolutely right. I couldn't less appreciate him.

I said "now I know why there wasn't a single paper containing Julia Wilson's original handwriting in her house. If you want to prove that the suicide note is originally Miss Julia Wilson's, then you have to remove all the documents and papers which actually have her original handwriting on. And I believe they intentionally kept the book list in Mr Carter's coat's pocket when they found it. So that we find it. Match the handwriting with the suicide note which proves that both are her handwriting."

"Well done my dear Watson. If you keep progressing like this, then in few days you will be one of the best detective England will ever get" Wilfred said with his usual sense of humour.

I said "Enough of your jokes Wilfred. Now please tell me why did you bring all the books here?"

In reply Wilfred gave me two copies of a same book. One from Miss Julia Wilson's collection and another one from his library and asked "Can you find any difference in between these two books?"

I looked with a lot of attention but didn't find anything.

He said "look carefully Richard. You will find something."

So, I started looking again and then automatically "my god" came out of my mouth. The first page is missing from Julia Wilson's book. It was cut so accurately, that no one will understand that page is not missing unless you have a great observation.

Wilfred said "I doubt this is not the only book where a page will be missing. There are more."

"Julia Wilson wrote something in all of these pages, right? That's why they were cut off" I said.

"Yes. I had been sure that this is exactly what happened. That's why I brought some of her books. If most of the pages of these books are torn, then our doubt is correct. She did write something in these pages. Now I think if you go to the J.C library in Julia Wilson's office, you won't find any document there either with her handwriting on it. Those also have been removed by now I believe" Wilfred said.

I said "but you could have done this in London in the J.C library. Why come here?"

He said "Richard, if a group of people are stealing books from the library for some reason, played Harold Carter against Julia Wilson and then eventually killed them both, what do you think will they not be from the inside of the library?"

My eyes widened. Yes, it has to be from inside. Who else will know where the books are better than someone or some people from in the library.

"That's why I don't want them to know that we found out that Julia Wilson was murdered and also, she was framed. If we would have brought Julia Wilson's books to the library to check with the other books, the killers would have understood that we know that Julia Wilson was murdered" Wilfred said.

I said "then we have to warn Dorothy about this. She might not know this. She could be in trouble."

Wilfred said "don't worry. I gave a hint to Raymond. He will take care of that. Alright, now check the books if there is any page missing."

We checked all the books. Some books had its front page or any page from the middle missing and some books were intact. It took near two hours to check all those books. It was 9.10 PM on the watch. I was looking at the threat letters which were given to Mr Carter. A lot of ideas were circling around my mind. I was trying to think like Wilfred. His process of detection and deduction is astonishing. He hardly had time to look at those threat letters and the book list. Yet he found out that the handwriting on the suicide note is different than the handwriting on the book list. He also found out the similarities in alphabets between the threat letters and the suicide note. And not only that, his doubt about Julia Wilson's car never left her garage is also making sense now. The more I was watching him the more I was getting fascinated.

Having a guess about what I was thinking, Wilfred said "It is not that hard Richard. Like I said you before. It is just observation. Watch and then create a theory. Then try to prove your theory."

"Does it work all the time?" I asked.

"Most of the time" Wilfred said.

"You said someone from inside had done this. Who that can be?" I asked.

"Someone who knew that both Mr Carter and Miss Wilson were investigating. Someone close to Miss Wilson. Who comes to your mind?" Wilfred asked.

"Flora? Goodness me. Apart from Mr Carter, she is the only person who remained close to Miss Wilson. And you said that she used to go to the library with Miss Wilson at night" I said.

Wilfred kept quiet for a minute and then smiled at me.

"But why Flora would do that?" I asked.

"I told you Richard when somebody does any illegal business, they don't care about their close ones" Wilfred said.

"But tell me this Wilfred, you said she was the first person to find out Miss Wilson was dead. If she killed Miss Wilson, then why did she go back to that place again? Because after a murder killer don't go back to the crime zone, do they?" I asked.

"Normally they don't but in some circumstances they do. She left something there Richard. She went again to take it" Wilfred said.

"What?" I asked.

"Not now Richard. Later" Wilfred said.

Wilfred remained quiet for sometimes. Then he said—

"When she went back for the second time, she couldn't hold her nerve because she didn't get what she was looking for. That's why she forgot the newspaper. She didn't drop it" Wilfred said.

"If your words are true Wilfred, then we have to catch her as early as possible. Because she already knows that we are doubting her."

"We will. Don't worry about that" Wilfred said.

"So at first they killed Mr Carter and then Julia Wilson?" I asked.

"Yes" Wilfred said.

"I don't think Julia Wilson had a clue that her best friend is the master mind behind this?" I asked.

"Certainly not. Otherwise, she would have taken steps and would have been alive" Wilfred said.

"Thank God that Julia Wilson is not involved on this. Because I think she was a nice person" I said.

Wilfred said "That is for sure. She was not behind all these. But unfortunately, both Mr Carter and Julia Wilson was doubting each other. Remember what Dorothy said. Mr Carter lied to Julia Wilson about disappearance of the books. I think when Mr Carter spotted that the books are disappearing, he decided to investigate and then if necessary, report this to the police. Somehow the criminals got to know about this and that decision of his scared the rats. Because if police get involved and an investigation starts, then there lies a chance of getting caught. So, they needed a solution and they came up with this master plan. They sent him threats letters. Warned him to stop. Because until then the killers didn't know that Mr Carter is doubting Julia Wilson.

But Mr Carter didn't stop. So, they killed him. The killer or killers made this plan very carefully. As we think of now that Flora is behind all these, she was sure that Mr Carter would never doubt her. And I think, may be Julia Wilson had told Flora that Mr Carter has started to doubt about the disappearances of the books. So, after killing Mr Carter Flora used the book list to stay safe. She killed Julia Wilson and wrote a suicide note by copying her handwriting."

"So they were building this plan for a long time?" I asked.

"Yes. It wasn't made overnight. Anyway, will you spend the night in my house? Or are you going to your place? Well, if you choose to stay in my house, I can help you out in one particular mater" Wilfred said.

"What matter?" I asked.

"I will inform you when Evelyn crosses my house tomorrow morning" Wilfred laughed.

"Damn you Wilfred. You are still joking after this serious conversation. And don't you remember, you are the one who told me to stay away from her. Damn you Wilfred" I said again.

"Good night. Off you go" Wilfred said.

I lay down on the floor.

Wilfred gave me a strange look and said "You are going sleep in the library?"

"Why? Is there a problem? I will not tear pages from your books" I said.

"My friend, why are you getting angry? I was just joking. I have a guest room in my house which I clean every day. So, it is ready to use. Please go there and sleep well and don't let Evelyn haunt you in your dream" Wilfred said in his naughtiest voice.

I threw my pen towards him and left the library.

The Man from the Petrol Pump

I woke up little late in the next morning and Evelyn did come to my dream last night. I was trying very hard to not to think about her but Wilfred intentionally pronounced her name in my ear and I started thinking about her again. When I came to drawing room Wilfred already finished his breakfast and was drinking coffee.

He looked at me said in his mockery voice "so, she did haunt you last night in your dream, didn't she?"

"How do you know that?" I asked in solemn face.

"Because you look depressed. You saw her in your dream and you were happy. But when you woke up you realized that you were dreaming and all the happiness has gone out of the window. That's why you are standing in front of me with this expressionless face. Anyway, did you share bed with her in your dream? Or just a kiss? Dear God, you did none of that. Really Richard? You couldn't even make love with her in your dream? Then what's the point of dreaming? Take my suggestion. Don't dream anymore. Such a shame."

I was standing and listening to Wilfred's mockery.

I said "You know Wilfred, there is one thing about you I have understood by now."

"And that is?" he asked.

I said "You may be a great detective and a musician but you know nothing about love."

"Really? How can you say that?" he asked.

I said "If you would, then you would never make fun of this matter."

"Ah Richard, I was just trying to bring some humour in your life" Wilfred said.

"By hurting my feelings? You know I won't get her. This case was helping me to get rid of that attraction I had of her and now you brought that back again. So kindly tell me my friend how are you bringing some humour into my life?" I asked.

"I am so sorry. I never thought it will be that serious" Wilfred said.

Though he said sorry but still I knew deep down in my heart he was enjoying every bit of it.

I said "That's alight. When do we leave?"

"As soon as you finish your breakfast and get ready" he said.

"I'm not hungry. Let's go" I said in a witty voice.

Wilfred said "I can understand your condition Richard, but never say no to food. Your situation will not change depending on whether you eat or not. And we are going to have a long and tiresome day today. Because I am about to unfold the mystery. So, you may not get another chance to eat in a while. So please eat."

"You found out the murderers?" I asked in excitement.

"Yes. But first eat and then we will run to London. The car is waiting outside" Wilfred said.

We reached London within four hours. Wilfred didn't talk in the entire journey. I tried my utmost best to make him say something but he was so stubborn that I failed miserably. I spent the entire journey by reading newspaper and watching the wonderful view of England. Upon reaching London at first, we went to the Scotland Yard. Raymond wasn't arrived yet. So, we were told to wait outside. I was staring at Wilfred and he was ignoring me like an unknown person. At some point I ran out of patient and was about to blast out my anger but right at that time Raymond arrived and saved the moment. Wilfred looked at me with a mockery face.

"Sorry to let you wait. Come inside" Raymond said.

We went inside his chamber.

"So, Wilfred what is your detection and deduction is saying?" Raymond asked.

"Miss Wilson didn't commit suicide. She was murdered" Wilfred said.

"Murder? What? But how? And what about the suicide note?" Raymond asked.

Wilfred explained everything to Raymond. He was listening with interest. As Wilfred was explaining everything to him, I saw nothing but expression of appreciation on his face. After all he knows Wilfred more than I do. There was silence for two minutes and satisfaction on Raymond's face. He backed up Wilfred's theory by tapping him on his back.

"Wow. Flora Rogers. I mean who would have thought that? The most trusted person and a best friend turned her back to her best friend. You know Wilfred because of this kind of situations it will be very hard to trust a person in future. Anyway, how do we catch her?" Raymond asked.

"We will. I have a plan. Not sure it will work but we will have to execute it" Wilfred said.

"What plan?" I asked.

"Will tell you that Richard but before that we have to inform Dorothy. Did she know about Miss Wilson's death?" Wilfred asked.

"Yes, I told her" Raymond said.

"And her reaction?" Wilfred asked.

"She wasn't ready to believe that Julia Wilson killed Harold Carter and committed suicide. I believe she is still not ready. She knows both of them better than anyone I suppose. And that's why from the get going she kept saying that Miss Wilson was not behind this and now your theory proves that she is right. Because as much as I was trying to convince her that indeed Miss Wilson committed suicide that much unconvincing, she was getting. She continuously said that Miss Wilson cannot commit suicide because she was absolutely fine and there is no chance that she killed Mr Carter" Raymond said.

"Yes, she was right. Right by trust. Anyway, we have to tell her everything. I don't know why I am getting a feeling that may be her life is in danger. That is why we have to warn her" Wilfred said.

"She might be at home right now. Because the library is closed" Raymond said.

"Do me a favour Raymond. Send someone to Dorothy's house and ask her to come to the library" Wilfred said. And then he turned towards me and asked—

"When was the last time you fired a gun?"

I was taken by surprised by that question. I said—

"Me?"

"You were in the army. When was the last time you fired a gun?" Wilfred asked again.

I said "A year or two perhaps."

"Are you expecting resistance" Raymond asked.

"Yes. Like I said Flora is not alone. We have to catch all of them. I don't think they will give up without a fight. So, we have to be prepared. I brought my gun. I don't think Richard did. Please give my Watson a gun inspector Lestrade" Wilfred said in delightful voice.

"This is the one thing I don't like about you Wilfred. You don't know where to crack a joke and when to crack a joke. We were talking about a serious matter.

And you are cracking jokes? And how many times did I tell you to not to call me Lestrade? I am way better than him Wilfred in thousand ways. He wasn't a police officer. He was a foolish officer" Raymond said.

Wilfred laughed so loud that at least four officers peeked in Raymond's chamber.

"Anyway, you are going to the library, right? Come to my place after that. My home will be your resting place for today. Don't worry Richard I do cook well. You will be delighted" Raymond said.

I shook his hand with a broad smile in my face and asked—

"And the gun?"

"I will give you that then" Raymond said.

We came out of the police station. A car was waiting to take us to the library.

Dorothy came ten minutes later after we reached the library. We were walking around the library from outside. She invited us inside. We went to Dorothy's office. Wilfred asked—

"How are you holding up?"

"Trying to fathom of what exactly happened. This is unbelievable isn't that Sir? Two of my closest person died in one night. And not only that, one of them has been charged with the murder of the other one. I don't think I will be able to accept this. Who is going to take care of this library now?" Dorothy was trying very hard to hold her tears.

I was feeling bad for her. This is true that Dorothy's responsibilities have gone mammoth in one night. Now she is the one who has to take care of this library.

Wilfred said "I have to tell you something Dorothy. Take a seat."

Dorothy sat down on a chair.

"Listen Dorothy, Julia Wilson didn't commit suicide and neither had she killed Harold Carter" Wilfred said.

Dorothy stood up from the chair and said—

"Are you sure about this? Because that's what I was trying to tell the inspector that Madam Julia didn't do this. She can't. Thank God."

"And not only that, but also she was not involved in the disappearance of the books" Wilfred said.

"So was she killed?" Dorothy asked.

"Yes Dorothy. They both were killed. Most probably by the same person" Wilfred said.

"Who did this?" Dorothy asked.

Wilfred didn't reply to Dorothy's question. Instead, he asked

"What do you think about Miss Flora Rogers?"

"Flora? She is a nice girl. But why are you asking this Sir?" Dorothy asked.

"We went to Flora's house yesterday to talk to her. She lied about two things. She was the first person to discover Miss Wilson's body but she didn't tell us" Wilfred said.

Dorothy was stunned. She said—

"Flora? What was she doing there? Because the police said that you were the first to discover Madam Julia's dead body."

"Yes. But she went before we went. And not only that. She lied about another thing. She told us that Julia Wilson used to go to the library in the middle of the night to investigate the ongoing matter. She said0 Julia Wilson used to go to the library alone and used to tell her about her findings. But according to me Flora used to go with her. I am telling this because I have proof. According to her Miss Wilson was supposed to go to the library on the same night she was killed. I believe Flora was also supposed to go with her. But I believe because of the rain Miss Wilson decided not to go. But according to a latter written by Harold Carter right before his death says that he saw Miss Wilson in the library. The woman she saw was wearing a dress which was gifted by Mr Carter. Now that can't be Miss Wilson because she didn't go to the library that night and I have evidences to prove that. But nevertheless, there was a woman who was wearing Miss Wilson's dress. What do you think Dorothy who that can be? Who had the most chance to know the where about of where Miss Wilson used to keep her things?" Wilfred asked.

"For that person who was very close to Madam Julia" Dorothy said.

"Not only close Dorothy. It was only possible for that person who used to go to her house quite often. There was three persons who were very close to Miss Wilson. Mr Carter, you and Flora. But among three of you Mr Carter and Flora used to go to her house very frequently. Just like Mr Carter Miss Wilson also used to share a lot of things with Flora. Now we can dismiss Mr Carter from the equation. So who is remaining?" Wilfred was spot on.

"Flora. My God" Dorothy said.

"Yes Flora. She knew where Miss Wilson kept her things" Wilfred said.

"So, she was the one who was stealing the books? And Madam Julia didn't know this?" Dorothy said.

Wilfred nodded his head.

"But how did she steal Madam Julia's dress? I mean to say how did she get in?" Dorothy asked.

"Thieves always have their ways to break into a house Dorothy. She must have stolen her dress when Miss Wilson wasn't home" Wilfred said.

"So, she wore that dress and went to the library. Mr Carter saw her but because of the dress he thought he saw Madam Julia. Bit how did she know that Mr Carter will go to the library that night?" Dorothy asked.

"I believe killing Mr Carter wasn't the plan. Flora used to go with Julia Wilson to check whether she was on the right track or not. This was important for Flora. Because if for once Flora could know that Julia Wilson found out something against her, then she would kill her. Now I believe Flora is not working alone. There are more in her group. I think Julia Wilson did find out something against one of her group members and told this to Flora. Because she had no idea that the person, she trusts is the one behind all these" Wilfred said.

"Goodness gracious me. Then?" Dorothy asked.

"I think Julia Wilson told Flora that Harold Carter is also has started doubting. This made Flora little bit reckless. So, she started to watch Mr Carter. Like I said Flora is not working alone. Murdering both of them wasn't possible for Flora. She had company. I believe the day Flora got to know that Harold Carter is also sticking his nose into this matter, she had told one of her colleagues to watch him twenty for hours. That's when they started to threaten him but that didn't work either. He didn't stop investigating. This decision of Mr Carter didn't leave Flora with any other choice but to kill him. And perhaps that person who was watching him informed Flora Mr Carter is going to the library. So, they killed him and then carried his dead body to Wiveliscombe.

After killing him they went to Julia Wilson's house and then killed her by poison. Then copied her handwriting to write the suicide note and left the place. But in the morning, she went back to Julia Wilson's house because she forgot something. Something that can be used against her as a proof. She went there to take it. But unfortunately, she didn't get what she was looking for and in panic she left valuable clue which led me to her" Wilfred said.

"What clue?" Dorothy asked.

"She dropped her newspaper there. Julia Wilson used to read The Times not The Herald. When we were searching her house, we didn't find a single Herald" Wilfred said.

"Yes. Madam Julia loved to read The Times" Dorothy said.

"Right. Now the question came into my mind is why all of a sudden someone would bother to buy The Herald when that person loves to read The Times? But when we went to Flora's house, we saw bunch of The Heralds but they were old. The current issue wasn't there. That proves that she went to Miss Wilson's house and in panic of not getting what she was looking for dropped the newspaper and left" Wilfred said.

"But why was she panicking?" Dorothy asked.

"She was afraid of getting caught. I just told you while ago Dorothy she must have left something which can lead us to her" Wilfred said.

"Did you get it?" Dorothy asked.

"Not yet. But I will find it. It is just a matter of time" Wilfred said.

"Still can't believe that Flora is behind all of this. Bit how will you catch her?" Dorothy asked.

"We have to find what she was looking for. But there is one more way. The dress. When we went to Mr Carter's house, I found a torn piece of cloth from a dress of a woman. That means Mr Carter resisted when Flora and her associates tried to kill him and that's when that little part of that dress was torn. Now we also searched Miss Wilson's house but we didn't find any dress which has a part missing. So I believe that dress is still in Flora's house unless she threw it away. If we can get that dress that will work as solid evidence against her." Wilfred said.

"But how will you get it?" Dorothy asked.

"Somehow, we need to bring her out of her house. Can you do that Dorothy? She is already doubting that we are onto her. If we go to her house, she will know this for sure and will try to get rid of the dress. If that dress goes away, she will walk free. Can you do that?" Wilfred asked.

"Of course, Sir. I would do anything to catch the killer of Madam Julia and Mr Carter" Dorothy said.

Wilfred smiled and said—

"Thank you, Dorothy. But did you think about one thing?"

"What?" Dorothy asked.

"You were supposed to go with Mr Carter to the library, right? Think about this. If you would have gone with Mr Carter that night, you wouldn't have been seating and talking with us right now. Flora would have killed you too" Wilfred said.

Dorothy severed for moment and her face became pale. She asked—

"Flora will not kill me in the day light, right?" Dorothy asked in trembling voice.

"Don't worry Dorothy. Flora is not that much stupid. You are safe in the day. Your only concern is in the night. Don't open the door to anyone. Unless it is me, Richard or Raymond. Even if someone says that he is from the police, still you won't open the door. Now go home and plan for tomorrow that how will you bring her out" Wilfred said.

Dorothy left the library.

We came out of the library. The police car was still waiting for us there. We get in the car and Wilfred said to the driver "Chiswell Street."

"Chiswell Street? Are we going to Miss Wilson's house" I asked.

"Not really. We are going to the petrol pump nearest to her house. Most probably ten minutes walking distance. Didn't you notice?" Wilfred said.

"Of course, I did. I have the ability to detect a petrol pump. You can't stay without mocking me right? I know I can't detect the way you do but I do write better than you" I said.

"Ah, Richard you are getting angry again. I did not mock you this time. I just asked" Wilfred said.

The driver was laughing listening to our conversation. The moment I looked at him he said—

"I beg a pardon Sir but I couldn't control."

"It is all right my friend. Anyway, now tell me Wilfred what will you in a petrol pump?" I asked.

"I need to talk to him. His name is David Brett. I believe he knew Miss Wilson very well and he had an affection for her" Wilfred said.

I said "How can you say that? You just seen him once. You haven't even talked to him".

"He was standing in the crowd when Raymond and four constables were taking out Miss Wilson's dead body, Remember? There was a reason why he grabbed my attention Richard" Wilfred stopped and looked at me.

"What reason?" I asked.

Wilfred said "Everyone was talking about how unfortunate Miss Wilson's death was but that man was mourning. I looked at him very carefully Richard. There was a disbelief and sadness in his eyes. I believe he couldn't believe the fact that Miss Wilson committed suicide and also couldn't believe the fact that he won't see Miss Wilson again."

"Is this the only reason to talk to him? Or there is more?" I asked.

Wilfred looked at me and said—

"What do you think?"

I said "I think there is more."

"Such as?" Wilfred asked.

I said "That petrol pump is on the road which goes directly to Miss Wilson's house. That means whether you want to go to her house or you want to go to somewhere else from her house, you have to cross that petrol pump. I think you want to ask him whether he saw Flora Rogers crossing that petrol pump going towards Miss Wilson's house in the middle of the night or not. Because if he did, then in that case we do have an eyewitness on favour of us."

Wilfred gave me an appreciative look. The driver said—

"Mr Wright has only told me that Mr Dankworth is a detective. But now it seems that you too is very good at detection Mr?"

"Bennett. Richard Bennett. Thank you very much. Now a days I very rarely see people is praising my detection and deduction process. So thank you once again. But who is Mr Wright?" I asked.

"This is your problem, Richard. Sometimes your deduction is mind blowing. But then you stumble onto little things. That is what disheartens me. Wright is Raymond's last name. I did mention you his full name when I told you about him for the first time. As usual you forgot" Wilfred said.

The driver started laughing again. All that happiness I felt because of his praising has now turned into disappointment. I kept quiet. It was near afternoon. The roads of London looked a bit busier than the other day. It took almost an hour to reach the petrol pump near Miss Wilson's house. Wilfred told the driver to park the car in front of Miss Wilson's house. A young boy was seating outside of the office. We walked towards him. Wilfred asked—

"Hello. Is Mr Brett in there? I need to talk to him"

"Are you from the police Sir? Because I saw you getting off from police car," said the young man.

"Not exactly. I am a private detective but sometimes I work Scotland Yard. Is he in there?" Wilfred asked again.

"Yes Sir. Wait here" the young man said and went inside the store. Five minutes later a gentleman came out. He was near fifty years old. He looked little devastated.

"How can I help you gentlemen?" he asked.

"We came here to ask you some questions about Miss Wilson's suicide" Wilfred said.

"I have said everything to the police already. Raymond Wright came here the day Julia died. I told him everything he wanted to know. Robert told me that you are a detective. If you are working with Scotland Yard then you should know what I told everything to Raymond Wright. Don't you people communicate with each other? I have nothing more to say. I am already in a very stressful mind about my work. So please stop bothering me."

Mr Brett stopped and started walking towards the store. Wilfred waited for few seconds and then said—

"Just like you I do believe that Miss Wilson didn't commit suicide. She was murdered."

Mr Brett stopped. I could see his right hand was shaking. He turned towards us and said—

"But you said to Robert that you work with the police. The police are saying that she committed suicide."

"I know. But I have a different view and I was able to convince Raymond about my theory" Wilfred said.

Mr Brett walked towards us and said—

"Alright. Ask me whatever you want to ask."

"Thank you, Mr Brett. How close were you with Miss Wilson?" Wilfred asked.

"Close? Why should I be close to her? She used to come here for to feel her car. That's how much I knew her" Mr Brett said.

"Don't test my ability of detection Mr Brett. I watched you very carefully yesterday when you were standing in the crowd. I saw a drop of tears in your eyes. Please help me to catch whoever killed Miss Wilson" Wilfred said.

Mr Brett took a deep breath and said—

"Julia was like daughter to me. She was a wonderful girl. She was very happy because of her relationship with Harold Carter. She respected and loved me as a father. She was planning to marry Harold Carter."

"What?" Both mine Wilfred's eyes become widened.

Wilfred said "But as far as I know for some reason Miss Wilson was denying Harold Carter's proposal of marriage."

"Yes. She was. But two days ago, before she died she said to me that she wants to marry Harold Carter. She is waiting for problem to be solved. Once it is solved, she will marry him. I asked her whether this problem was about relationship or not. In that case I could help her. But she said it was not about relationship. It was something else. She said she will surprise Harold Carter. Now you tell me how can a girl who is very happy because she is about to marry her lover, killed her love and then committed suicide? How in the world this is possible?"

The news of Miss Wilson about to marry Mr Carter was entirely new to us.

"Did she talk about this with anyone except you?" Wilfred asked.

"No. I was the only one knew about this," said Mr Brett.

"Alright Mr Brett. I want you to think about the night when both Miss Wilson and Mr Carter died. It was raining heavily all night long. Now tell me did you see Miss Wilson's car crossing your petrol pump in between 11.30 to 12 AM?" Wilfred asked.

"How do I know? I was sleeping. Don't you see I am fifty years old" Mr Brett said.

Wilfred gave him a smile and said—

"No Sir. You were not sleeping. In fact, you don't sleep in the night. Because you are suffering from insomnia."

Mr Brett seemed impressed by Wilfred's reply. He asked—

"How do you know?"

"Those dark circles under your eyes. It is a clear sign that you don't sleep in the night. So, you saw everything. Now please tell me did you see Miss Wilson's car crossing your petrol pump in the night she died?" Wilfred asked again.

"No. After coming back from the library she didn't come out of her house" Mr Brett said.

"Alright. That make sense. Now tell me did you see any other car going towards her house and coming back in between 1 to 3 AM?" Wilfred asked.

I saw a spark in the eyes of Mr Brett. His eyes were shining. He said—

"Yes, my son. One car went towards her house came back in between the time you said."

"Were you able to see who were in the car? All I am asking did see you any woman inside the car?" Wilfred asked.

"Yes. There was a woman inside the car. The car came here and stopped. A man got out of the car came to my store asking for bandage. I was sitting inside the office. I couldn't see his face. He was wearing a raincoat and trying to cover his face. I took a little time to find the bandage. When I handed the bandage to that man right then another car came for fuel. The headlight of that car was on. And right then for a glance I saw a woman sitting in the car which came before. Without that headlight it would have been impossible to spot her" Mr Brett said.

"Was she bleeding?" Wilfred asked.

"Well, I don't think I will be able to answer that question. I saw her for a glance. It was impossible to see whether she was bleeding or not. But it is also possible that maybe that woman or that man was bleeding. Otherwise, why would he have asked for a bandage" Mr Brett said.

"Did you see the time?" Wilfred asked.

"Not exactly. But it was after 2 AM. Because at 2 AM I went to the bathroom. So, I remember the time" Mr Brett said.

"If I show you that woman again, will you be able to recognise her?" Wilfred asked.

"I think I will" Mr Brett said.

"Thank you, Mr Brett. That will be all. We may need your assistance tomorrow" Wilfred said.

"Did they kill Julia?" Mr Brett asked.

"I can't say for sure but I am working on it" Wilfred said.

"What is your name son?" Mr Brett Wilfred asked.

"Wilfred Dankworth" Wilfred said.

"And you?" Mr Brett asked me.

I said "my name is Richard Bennett."

"Are you, his assistance?" Mr Brett asked.

I smiled and said "sort of."

Mr Brett looked at Wilfred and said—

"Mr Dankworth if anybody can solve this mystery is you. Mr Wright didn't ask me these questions. That car was the only car which went towards Julia's house and came back during that entire night. The car came later took petrol and went back to where it came from. Then in the morning when I heard about Julia's death, I started to doubt that may be that car had something to do with it. Because Mr Wright said Julia committed suicide around 2 AM. So that car's going towards her house before 2 AM. Then coming back after 2 AM. And then that man asking for bandage created a good bit of doubt in my mind. Because I knew Julia can't commit suicide. I wanted to tell all of these to the police but they didn't ask me anything about this. And I also was a bit afraid that if I tell them all these things, maybe they will involve me into the matter. So, I kept my mouth shut. Please catch them Mr Dankworth."

"I will Mr Brett. I will" Wilfred said.

Our work was done here. It was almost 4 PM. We both were hungry. So, we started going towards Raymond's house.

Three Bullets and a Man Down

Raymond was waiting for us at the drawing of his house. He watched us coming. So, before we even knock, he opened the door himself and came outside and said—

"Where the hell have you been? It is 4.30. I was waiting for both of you almost an hour now."

"Sorry Raymond. We had some work to do" Wilfred said.

"Yes, I know that. Anyway, tell me what you got" Raymond said.

Wilfred told everything to him. Raymond was taken by surprise after hearing what David Brett had said to us. He said—

"To be honest with you Wilfred I would have never found out that Miss Wilson was murdered. It is you who found that out. See that is why I involved you in this case. Because from the get going I knew this won't be easy. We get lots of cases every week. But killing someone in London and then dumped his body to Wiveliscombe is not normal. And this is why I needed your help. Without you this case would not have been solved. We would have closed the case by saying that

Miss Wilson murdered Harold Carter and committed suicide. Anyway, now tell me what the plan is"

"Alright. Listen carefully. I and Richard will spend the night in Miss Wilson's house. I am expecting a guest or guests there tonight" Wilfred said.

"Flora?" I asked.

"Flora won't come. She will send someone else to get the job done. They left something in that house and they will take a chance to get it tonight and that's when we have to catch them. Richard, you will stay near Dorothy's house. Though I told her to stay inside but still there is a possibility that Flora or her associates may take chance to take her out. So, you stay there. Don't go alone. Take some of your men with you. This can be a long night. So, we better get some rest" Wilfred said.

"Alright. Let's eat first. Then I will go to the station. I have to inform my men" Raymond said.

We were so hungry that finished our lunch within ten minutes. Raymond was about to leave, right then Wilfred said—

"You take rest Richard. Try to sleep a little. Like I said it will be a long night. I am going out with Raymond. I will be back in ten minutes."

Wilfred went outside. The bed was prepared. I wanted to wait for Wilfred to come but the bed looked so alluring that I couldn't resist myself. And also, I was feeling very tired. It has been a while since I left army.

That physical strength and energy what I used to have has gone now. So, I was feeling very much sleepy. I immediately lied down on the bed and put my head on a nice and soft pillow. I think just before I fell asleep, I heard Raymond said "What?" The next thing I remember is Wilfred was trying to wake me up.

"Richard, wake up. We have to get ready" Wilfred said.

I sat up on the bed. It was nine o clock in the night. I said—

"Are you sure they will come? Because we still have police protection there. I don't think they will take any chance."

"Yes, my dear Richard they will take this chance. I asked Raymond to move some of his men from there and keep only one officer. The murderers will see this as an opportunity. So, they will definitely come" Wilfred said.

"So, if we can catch them then it will be easy to relate Flora with this murder. Right?" I asked.

"Of course. But we also need proof against her. And this where Dorothy will come handy. She will bring Flora outside somehow and I will break into her house to grab the dress" Wilfred said.

"But what if burned it or threw it somewhere else? Then what proof shall we have?" I asked.

"Let's hope that she didn't burn that dress and still kept it in her house" Wilfred said.

I was looking at Wilfred because I was not feeling confident about this plan of his. I said—

"You know Wilfred till now I was pretty much confident about everything you were doing. I never doubted on your detection and deduction process. But these two plans of yours, seems like you made these plans based on luck. Because I am not seeing any guarantee of success. What if Flora's associates don't come tonight and what if you don't get the dress in Flora's house? Then what?"

Wilfred smiled and said—

"Don't worry Richard. Everything will happen as planned. I know my plans raised some questions in your mind but trust me Richard these plans are not based on luck. Just wait for a while you will get to know everything" Wilfred said.

Though Wilfred was trying to convince me about the success rate of his plans but my doubts were not going. A half an hour later Raymond came with a gun. It was a Smith and Wesson .38 long colt revolver. I have used this revolver during World War two. So, I was familiar with it. Raymond asked—

"I think you have used this revolver before, right?"

"Yes. I did" I said and I then turned towards Wilfred and said—

"I won't let you down Wilfred. And if I get the chance to show you how good I am in shooting, then I am not going to let that opportunity go away from me."

"Seems like the solider has come back again inside you" Wilfred said.

I smiled and said "well it is a question about a murderer. Though I want to leave in piece but still I can't let a crime unpunished. Don't forget I fought for my country and I killed for my country."

"Alright, let's discuss the plan. Listen Richard, we won't go directly to Miss Wilson's house by car. We will get out of the car a bit before her house and will walk on foot to the petrol pump station. Raymond has already informed Mr David Brett. He will help us. The petrol pump will be closed tonight and all the lights will be turned off. We will stay there till 11.30 PM. Right now, three police officers are guarding the house. Exactly at 11.30 PM two of them will leave. They will cross the petrol pump by foot. As soon as we see them, we will start walking towards Miss Wilson's house. We will go inside the house and will wait for the killers or one of the killers. I don't think they will come before 12.30 or 1 AM. Once we settle down in our hiding positions the remaining one police officer will start patrolling the street. We can't remove him from there. Because the case isn't solved yet and we know how cunning these criminals are. So if we move every police officer from there, the killers might doubt that they are walking into a trap and we can't take that risk. That's why instead of leaving the place that police officer will patrol in the street. The idea is that he will stay visible in the street but away from Miss Wilson's house. His absence in front of Miss Wilson's house will give the intruders a significant time to break into the house but his presence on the street will not create any doubt in their minds. And as soon as they get inside the house, we will pound on them. Clear?" Wilfred asked.

"Yes, my friend. Clear like day light" I said.

Then Wilfred turned towards Raymond and said—

"You and one of your men will wait near to Dorothy's house. Try to find a place where neither Dorothy nor anyone coming to her house will be able to see both of you. They may take an attempt to kill her and will try to make it look like a natural death. Though that chance is very little. Because I don't think Flora is that much stupid to take any risk like that. Because she knows that we all are doubting her. So, I don't think that she will take any chance but still for assurance that Dorothy stays alive you have to stay there."

"Understood" Raymond said.

"Alright, did you bring the dresses?" Wilfred asked to Raymond.

"Yes. Two black shirts and black hats" Raymond said.

"Black shirts and black hats? What will we do with them?" I asked.

Wilfred said "Richard, we will be hiding in the dark and what colour could be better than black to blend in with the darkness. Though we are dressed in black but our shirts are white and we didn't bring our hats. It will be cold in the night. A little protection. And one more thing Richard. I know how keen you are to showcase me how good you are in shooting and in aiming but please remember this Richard the place we are about to go is a residential area. So, if by any chance the criminal or criminals escape from us, then they could get into one of the houses for cover. In that case please don't shoot blindly. We will only shoot when we have a clear shot."

I was little angry hearing this. I said—

"You didn't need to say that to me Wilfred. I was a soldier. I had the responsibility to protect my country. At least I have that common sense when to shoot and when not to. I will never shoot a common person."

"Why are you getting angry Richard? I know you have that sense" Wilfred said.

"Really? You knew? If you knew then you wouldn't have said that. And if you said this jokingly, then my friend you can make fun of me about my detection power but not my shooting ability" I said angrily.

"There was a reason why I said this Richard" Wilfred said.

I said "I know why you said it. Because I had retired from army four years ago and spent my life in peace till now. So, it has been a while that I didn't get any taste of action and adventure. So, once I get an opportunity like this, I will be very much excited and will lose control on my nerve and will fire blindly. This is what you meant right Wilfred?"

Wilfred looked at Raymond. Raymond was enjoying our conversation. Finally, he said—

"For the first time I am watching somebody kept Wilfred's mouth shut. Well done Richard. He is right Wilfred. You didn't need to tell him about those rules. We were taught these rules in armed forces. Anyway, let's take the dinner and then get ready for action."

Around 10.30 PM I and Wilfred started going towards Miss Wilson's house and Raymond with one of his men went towards Dorothy's house. Raymond arranged a car for us as usual. This is the same driver from the morning. He will go back to the station after dropping us near petrol pump. Wilfred didn't speak a word in the car. His eyes were sparkling. His jaws became tight. I could see it. Raymond told me about this condition of Wilfred. The best way to describe this is like when the hunter finally knows who to hunt and where to hunt. When Wilfred is about to catch a criminal, his entire focus stays on one point. He forgets everything what's happening around him. Raymond had this kind of experiences before. This was the first time for me. All he told me was not to bother Wilfred when he is not talking and I obeyed Raymond's order. After going for some twenty to twenty-five minutes, the driver stopped the car. He said—

"The petrol pump is fifteen minutes away from here and Miss Wilson's house is approximately twenty-five to thirty minutes."

We started walking. I was feeling the excitement in my nerves. After long time I am about to serve my country again. Although most of the work was done by Wilfred but I was getting happy thinking that I will contribute to this noble work. At least our efforts will decrease one or two or maybe three criminals out of the streets. We were walking little faster than the normal speed. So, we reached the petrol pump station within ten minutes. As decided the petrol pump is closed and all the lights were turned off. Only the street lights were turned on. I saw a sign board kept at the entry point of the petrol pump with a message—

"Closed for repairing."

Wilfred stopped near the sign board. Watched the entire place very carefully and then started walking towards the office room. As soon as we reached near the office room a torch was turned on and then immediately turned off. Wilfred raised his right hand. A minute later Mr Brett came out. He was also wearing a black overcoat and a black trouser.

"Come in" he said in a very low voice.

Wilfred looked at his pocket watch. It was 11.25 AM. Approximately after five to ten minutes two policemen will cross the petrol pump as they were instructed before. And then we will start walking towards Miss Wilson's house. We went inside Mr Brett's office room. Mr Brett said—

"Raymond didn't tell me about your plan. I do know why and I respect that. How long will you be here?"

"Five to ten minutes maximum. Two police officers will cross your petrol pump. As soon as they cross, we will leave" Wilfred said.

"I really want to help both of you but as you see I am a bit old. I am afraid I will slow you down" Mr Brett said.

"You are already helping Mr Brett. If you hear gun shots, come to Miss Wilson's house. I will show one of the men who killed Miss Wilson" Wilfred said.

I was listening to their words but my eyes were on the streets. A few minutes later I saw two police officers crossing the petrol pump. One of them coughed a little louder.

"There goes our signal. They are leaving. It is time Richard. Alright Mr Brett, we are leaving. Be alert. If we can't catch him and he tries to run through your station you take him down" Wilfred said.

"That goes without saying son. I will take him down if he tries to go through here. Good luck," said Mr Brett.

We came out of the office room very carefully.

Wilfred said "try to avoid the street lights as much as possible Richard. It is better to stay in the dark."

So, we were walking avoiding the streets light as much as possible. Wilfred was watching the entire place. Very soon we reached Miss Wilson's house. One police officer was standing near a police car. He moved his head down like bowing after watching us and then moves his head side wise once. In reply Wilfred also moved his side wise.

"No one is here. Let's get inside. We will wait in Miss Wilson's bedroom. After five minutes Officer Dunn will lock the door from outside and start patrolling on the street" Wilfred said.

We went inside Miss Wilson's house and went straight to her bed room. Wilfred sat in a corner of the room on the floor left to the door. He can't be seen unless someone turns his or her head to the left. I went to seat beside the left side of the bed. A few minutes later officer Dunn locked the door form outside. Then he left for patrolling the street and the waiting game has begun. It was 11.55 PM on the clock when Officer Dunn left. I tried to calm myself down. Nothing happened in the next one hour and then I started to get restless. I was looking at the watch pretty frequently. Wilfred understood what I was going through. He gestured me to calm down. We waited for another hour. It was 2.15 AM on the clock and I started to fall asleep, right then Wilfred whispered—

"Richard. Someone is coming."

I woke up in a hurry tried to listen.

"Footsteps. Listen carefully" Wilfred whispered again

Now I could listen. But that man or woman hadn't entered in the house yet. Then I heard the sound of unlocking the door. All my nerves kicked in again. I was boiling in excitement from inside. That person opened the door and came inside the house. Now the sounds of footsteps became clearer. That person stopped at the drawing room. As in he or she was trying assess the environment. Then he started to come towards the bedroom. The door of the bedroom was also locked. After few minutes the door of Miss Wilson's bed room made a metallic sound. That means the door has been unlocked. I put my right hand in side my pocket and took the revolver out and aimed towards the door. Wilfred was also pointing his gun towards the door. I quickly but noiselessly moved under the bed and rolled onto the other side. The door was slowly opened. A man walked into the room. Though I was lying under the bed watching his feet size I realised that man is near six feet tall. He turned on his torch and pointed it right on left side of the door.

"Surprised?" Wilfred said and right then I rolled out underneath the bed, stood up on my feet and pointed the gun at that man. At first, he didn't understand what happened. But then he realised that he walked into a trap. He quickly drew the knife from his pocket and threw it at Wilfred and Wilfred screamed fell and down on the floor. The man started running. Even in that pain Wilfred shouted—

"Go after him Richard. Don't let him get away."

But that was not necessary. I was already started running after him. I ran as fast as I could and came out of the house chasing him. He was a few meters ahead of me. All my training from the army came into play. I was about to increased my speed, right then I heard Wilfred's voice. He was running behind me.

"Fire Richard. Take him down" Wilfred shouted.

I sat down on one knee and fired three times and all of the three bullets pierced into that man's right leg. Though it was only the street lights which were helping me but I was taught to hit the target in the dark during my army days. So, my bullets didn't miss the target. The man fell down on the street face first and started screaming in agonising pain. By this time Wilfred came beside me. He pulled me up and said—

"Good shot captain. Now come on."

We went to that man. He was suffering from excruciating pain. Wilfred sat on his chest and took something out of his pocket, showed it to that man and asked—

"This is what you came for right? Well, I had this from day one. Your master mind did understand but a little late."

"Are you alright Sir?"

I turned back. It was Officer Dunn. He came with more police officers. The sound of three bullets attracted the attention of a lot of people. Lights were turned on in every house and crowd started to gather on the street. Everyone was keen to know what happened. Officer Dunn tackled the situation wonderfully. I looked at Wilfred. He was bleeding from his hand.

"You are bleeding Wilfred. You need treatment immediately" I said.

"It is just a cut Richard. Don't worry" Wilfred said.

One Officer walked towards us and said—

"Mr Brett wants to see you."

"Let him through" Wilfred said.

The police mean created a circle around where the incident took place. Mr Brett was standing there. Wilfred waved his hand to him. One police officer let him through. He slowly walked towards us and asked—

"Did you catch the murderer?"

"Yes Mr Brett. We did. Actually, he did" Wilfred pointed his finger to me.

Mr Brett looked at me and asked—

"So, you fired those three shots?"

"Yes Sir" I said.

"But Mr Brett, this man is one of the murderers. There is two more. But don't worry we will catch them" Wilfred said.

"You are bleeding my son" Mr Brett said.

"That's just a cut" Wilfred said.

"Still, that's a wound. Come to my office. I have some bandage and iodine there. That will help to stop the blood" Mr Brett said.

"Alright Mr Brett. You go ahead. We are coming" Wilfred said.

Mr Brett turned towards me, tapped my back and said—

"Well done son" and started walking towards his petrol pump.

Officer Dunn was standing nearby. He came to us and said—

"Chief Inspector Wright told me about you Mr Bennett. Well, you certainly proved that you were in the army. All of three bullets went inside his leg. But the thing which is overwhelming me is you hardly had any light in the street but you still were able to aim at his leg. Unbelievable Sir. I have seen some of the best shootings in life and I was involved in some. But I have seen nothing like what you have just done."

"Thank you, Officer Dunn. In my military days I was even better" I said.

Wilfred said "take this man to the hospital. Don't need to inform Raymond yet. He is busy in another work. We are going to Mr Brett's office. I need to put some iodine and bandage on this wound. Can you arrange a car for to ride home?"

"Of course, Sir. You go to Mr Brett's office. I will send a car for you" Officer Dunn said.

"Thank you, officer," Wilfred said.

Mr Brett was waiting outside of his office. Now all the lights were turned on the station. The entire Chiswell Street has witnessed one of the most breath-taking incidents. Mr Brett poured some iodine onto Wilfred's wound and put a bandage there. Then he asked—

"Is that man and that woman who came to my petrol pump on the night of Julia's murder, are the rest of the murderer you were talking about?"

Wilfred nodded his head said—

"Yes. Alright, listen Mr Brett. I will be needing you tomorrow around 11.30 AM in Harold Carter's house. A police car will come and pick you up."

"But why?" asked Mr Brett.

"Because I am about to unfold the mystery and your presence is necessary. Because you are the only one who saw the murderers. Though I have solid proof against them but still you have to be present there" Wilfred said.

"Alright son. I will be on time" Mr Brett said.

The police car was waiting to take us home. Wilfred was humming a tune of his own. I laid flat on the bed once we reached Raymond's house. I was feeling very tired. Both physically and mentally. Because after a long time I went through this kind of excitement and physical exertion. But one thing I didn't understand. Wilfred said to Mr Brett that he will unfold the mystery tomorrow. So, I asked him—

"You said to Mr Brett that you will unfold the mystery tomorrow. But what mystery? We already know that Flora Rogers is behind all of this. Then what mystery is left to unfold?"

Wilfred took out something from his pocket. Then showed it to me and asked—

"Do you remember this?"

I couldn't remember whose it is. I said—

"I can't remember."

"Try to remember Richard. This is what the criminal came for. Think harder" Wilfred said.

Then all of a sudden everything came into mind. I jumped of the bed and said—

"My God. This is…" I couldn't speak.

"Yes my friend. I knew this from the first day once I got this" Wilfred said.

"But why didn't you tell this to me? Why did you wait for today? We already had the proof." I asked.

I will explain everything tomorrow. Now sleep until Raymond comes.

The Meeting

I slept pretty well last night. Because I couldn't remember when Raymond came. I woke up pretty late this morning again just like yesterday. It was 9.30 AM on the clock. Wilfred was reading The Herald. I asked—

"Did they publish the last night's incident?"

"Yes. They did. It is in the front page" Wilfred said and have the newspaper to me.

"They wrote my name. Who told them my name?" I asked and looked at Wilfred.

He was smiling. I asked—

"You told Raymond, right?"

"Yes, my dear Richard" Wilfred said.

"But why? I don't want to come into the spotlight. My days of fighting is over Wilfred. Yesterday was an exception. Well, if you think practically then it was not yesterday. Because the incident happened after midnight. But still today's incident or yesterday's incident whatever you call it was an exception. Because I don't think that all the cases you are going to solve next will have this much of shooting. I am a writer now Wilfred. I don't want to be in the spotlight" I said.

"You deserve it my friend. Because without you todays or yesterday's mission would not have been successful. You are the one who chased down the criminal not me. I was down on the floor. So, this country and its public needs to know about their saviour. I did the right thing. And who told you that my next cases will not be this much complicated. You never know" Wilfred said.

I was watching him. I know when he really praises somebody by his heart and this time he was praising me by his heart. I was happy because I was able to contribute in the safety of my country.

"Freshen up Richard and eat the breakfast. I have eaten mine. Raymond has already gone to Harold Carter's house. I think the guests have started to come. It is the climax Richard and it will be dramatic just like Sir Arthur Conan Doyle's or Agatha Christie's murder mystery" Wilfred said in a stagy manner.

"But what about Dorothy? You told her to bring out Flora from her house so that you can break in" I said.

"She had been informed. Raymond sent one of his men to her house to tell her to be present at Harold Carter's house at 10.30 AM. She will come in a police car. Because after last night's incident it is pretty much risky to leave her alone in the road. So, she will come with that police officer" Wilfred.

"Alright give me twenty minutes. I will be ready by then" I said and went to the bathroom.

We reached Harold Carter's house before 10.30 AM. All the guests were arrived by then. We all gathered in

Mr Carter's drawing room. Everyone looked a little discomfort. Specially Mr David Brett. I can understand his reason to be discomfortable. Because by now he had recognised the woman he saw at the night of Miss Wilson's death. Only Dorothy looked a little confident. Maybe because she knew who the murderer is. Wilfred waited for few minutes and then he started speaking—

"Good morning, everybody. The reason all of you are here because I am about to unfold the truth about Mr Harold Carter and Miss Julia Wilson's death and all of your presence is necessary. I have spoken to all of you. So by now you know who I am. But for your knowledge let me tell you again that why and how I got myself involved in this case. My name is Wilfred Dankworth. I am a guitarist and a private detective. Scotland Yard's chief inspector Raymond Wright is my dearest friend. He is the one who brought this case to me because it all started right where I live, Somerset Wiveliscombe. But before I tell you the real truth behind Mr Harold Carter and Miss Julia Wilson's death, there is a big story you have to know.

Now all of you know that Harold Carter was the owner of J.C library and Julia Wilson was the secretary of that library. Mr Carter and Miss Wilson were in a relationship for quite a long time and their lives were full of love and happiness until a strange incident started to happen inside the library. Miss Wilson was the first to discover that. She found out that for some reason some books from the library were disappearing themselves and also were coming in the next few days themselves. Now that is impossible. Books can't disappear themselves unless someone disappear them intentionally. Miss Wilson was a very clever and prudence person. She understood that fact pretty quickly that someone is intentionally disappearing those books. But why?

It is impossible to take book home because that facility had been closed for a long time. And it is also impossible to steal books from the library because a guard always check every reader before they enter and leave the library because of some past incidents of book stealing. So, Julia Wilson understood that this was not any ordinary incident. Someone for some purpose is behind this strange incident. So she decided to find more about this. She did not involve Harold Carter into this matter because she loved him a lot and she never wanted to bring any tension to his life. But Miss Wilson did have a partner to discuss about this matter. Flora Rogers. Flora is a reader of J.C library and very dear friend of Miss Wilson. Miss Wilson discussed this matter with her and understood that the disappearing of these books is not happening inside the library hours or in the day light. This is happening into the night after the library hours.

So, she decided to go to the library in the night to find out actually what was going on. In the meantime, Harold Carter also got to know about the disappearances of the books. But at that point of time Harold Carter had no idea why and who is doing this. And just like Miss Wilson, Mr Carter decided not to involve Miss Wilson into this matter for the same reason. Now six days ago Harold Carter and Julia Wilson spent a wonderful night together. This was two days before their death. In the next day Miss Wilson didn't come to the library. So, after waiting for a while Mr Carter decided to visit her place. In Miss Wilson's house he found a piece of paper with names of some books. He studied that book list and understood some of those books in fact all of those books once disappeared and came back. At first, he could not understand what this book list was doing in Miss Wilson's house and how she got it.

But immediately something worked in his mind. So, he left her place and came to the library with a lot of questions. As he was about to get off from his car, he saw a piece of paper on his car's back seat. He read the piece of paper and got stunned. It was a threat letter. It said—

'Stay of out of whatever is happening in the library. Don't try to contact the police. Else you will be dead'.

Harold Carter was heartbroken. Because by then he had no doubt that somehow Julia Wilson is involved in the disappearances of these books. He couldn't accept this fact. So he told one of the reader from the library to inform Dorothy that he is feeling sick and he is going home. She should come to his house after closing the library. Dorothy went to Mr Carter's house after closing the library and Mr Carter explained her everything. Dorothy did accept about the disappearance of the books but she was not ready to believe that Miss Wilson was behind this. Mr Carter asked Dorothy that how she knows about the disappearance of the books. In reply Dorothy said that she spotted this strange incident a while ago. Mr Carter was very much upset. So, Dorothy told him take care of himself and about to leave and right then both of them heard a sound of glass being broken. The sound came from the drawing room. Dorothy went to check and found that someone threw a piece of paper wrapped onto a stone through the window. She took that piece of paper to Mr Carter and told him how this got into his house. Mr Carter read the letter and started to shiver. Because that was another threat letter. It said—

'Stop doing your own investigation. I will not harm you unless you do something silly. And don't inform the police. Else there will be consequences.'

This threat letter made Harold Carter more determined to find whether Miss Wilson is really behind this or not. On the other hand, Mr Carter's strange behaviour put a doubt in Miss Wilson's mind. She started to believe that somehow Mr Carter found out about the disappearances of the books. So, she interrogated him but somehow Mr Carter was able convince her that he knows nothing. Now this was the incident of the day when Mr Carter died. Miss Wilson came to his house to ask all these questions. Then they both went to the library together. On that same day Mr Carter asked Miss Wilson to spend the night with him. But Miss Wilson declined his request by saying that she has to go to see the doctor because her friend Flora is suffering from fever and there is no one to help her. Now Mr Carter knew Flora only by her name. Despite of being his lover's dearest friend he never remembered how Flora looked like. Now later in the day Mr Carter found out that Miss Wilson was lying. Because on that same day Flora was present in the library and was not looking sick at all. Dorothy verified this. Right Dorothy?"

Wilfred turned towards Dorothy. Dorothy nodded her by saying yes. Wilfred started to speak again—

"After this lie Mr Carter became absolutely sure that Miss Wilson is behind all of this. But he needed proof. So, without informing Dorothy, he decided to go to the library in midnight on that very day. And as planned he went to the library in the midnight. He went inside and saw Miss Wilson going out of the library. He didn't see her face because it was very dark but he recognised her by her dress. That was the dress Mr Carter gifted Miss Wilson. Naturally he was heartbroken and came back to his house. He had proof but his heart stopped him to go to the police. He wanted to bring Miss Wilson out this matter. So, he wrote a letter addressing her. I found this letter from his study room. The letter says—

'Julia, I never ever thought you can do this to me. I loved you from the bottom of my heart. I gave you everything you ever needed and wanted from me and yet you betrayed me. You thought I didn't notice about what is going on in the library. But you were wrong

Julia Wilson. I knew everything but I never thought you are the one behind all this. When I went to your house two days ago, I saw a piece of paper on your desk containing the names of those books which had been disappeared and came back mysteriously. It was your handwriting, Julia Wilson. On that same day I got two threat letters because I was sticking my nose into the matter and started investigating on my own. Even yesterday evening when I asked to come with me to my home, you lied to me saying that you need to take Flora to the doctor. You said she was suffering from fever. You knew that I don't remember Flora's face. So, you took the chance. But the matter of fact is Flora was present on that day wasn't ill at all. But even after all these, I still didn't believe that you are involved in this matter. But now I am. I saw you tonight, Julia Wilson. I went to the library tonight to find out are you really involved or not. I saw you coming down from the second floor. What were you doing there in the middle of the night? Stealing another book? I know you are not doing this alone. Maybe you have been pressurised by someone. Because I know you can't do this to me. Please tell me who is forcing you to do this? There is still a way-out Julia Wilson. It is still not late. Don't talk to me about this. Maybe they are watching and listening. Write to me. Let me help you. Harold.'

I believe right after writing this letter Mr Carter died. According to me there was more than one person. They killed Mr Carter and then carried his dead body by a car to Somerset Wiveliscombe and dropped his body in the banks of the river Tone. A fisherman found his dead body and contacted the local police station and they contacted Scotland Yard later. Chief inspector Raymond came to Wiveliscombe and informed me about the matter. I, Richard and Raymond went to the place and I found out that Mr Carter was murdered. At the beginning I didn't recognise him but his face looked familiar to me. But later I recognised him. As he was from London, we started our journey towards here. By the time we reached London, Dorothy already filed a missing person's report.

Well, we informed Dorothy about the sad demise of his chief librarian and asked her if she knows anything and if she doubts anybody. Dorothy told everything about Mr Carter. How he got involved into this and why he was doubting Miss Wilson. From there we went to Miss Wilson's house. Because she didn't know about the death of Mr Carter. We went to inform her. But unbelievably we found her dead in her bed room with a suicide note. The suicide note said—

'I killed Harold. He was creating problem in my business. He was asking too many questions. He even told Dorothy about the disappearance of the books. I tried to keep him out of this. I even threatened him with a letter but he didn't listen to me. So he left me with no choice but to kill him. I never wanted to do this. But now I can't sleep. He was the only person who cared about me and I killed him. I can't stay here alone. I am going to meet him now. Burry my body beside him. I hope he forgives me, Julia Wilson.'

Though this suicide note was there but I was convinced by some proofs that Miss Wilson did not commit suicide. She was also murdered. Most probably by the same person who murdered Mr Carter. I also had proof then and there that Miss Wilson did not kill Harold Carter. The moment I understood this I told Richard and Raymond to search the house. We didn't get everything what we were looking for except a newspaper. The Herald. I picked up the newspaper, gave it to Richard and from there we went to Mr Carter's house. When we reached his house, it was a mess. It looked like someone searched the entire house for something. There I found the book list what Mr Carter found from Miss Wilson's house and the letter Mr Carter wrote before his death. Though the handwriting on the suicide notes and the book list was similar still I was not convinced. From there we went to Flora's house and that's when I discovered an untold truth. When I asked Flora what her thought about Miss Wilson's suicide, she said Miss Wilson can't commit suicide. She was killed because just like Harold Carter she was also investigating. That's why she was murdered. Then I asked Flora a few more questions and she answered properly except one thing."

Wilfred stopped and looked towards Flora.

Too Much Cunning Overreaches Itself

Flora was looking at the floor. Now she looked up and stared into the eyes of Wilfred and said—

"What are you talking about? I told you everything you wanted to know."

"You hide two truths from me Flora" Wilfred said.

"What truth?" Flora asked.

"You didn't tell me that you were the first person to discover Miss Wilson's death" Wilfred said in a cold voice.

I don't know for sure but I think Wilfred's statement shook flora's hand a little. She looked towards everyone in the room, closed her eyes and said—

"How did you know?"

"Because of this newspaper" Wilfred said and showed the newspaper to everybody.

Flora looked at Wilfred with a lot of questioned in her eyes. There was no doubt that she was taken by surprise by Wilfred's words.

"You dropped this newspaper in Miss Wilson's bedroom. And the second truth which you hid from me is that Miss Wilson never went to the library alone. You used to go with her. The way you explained every detail about the disappearances of those books is not possible unless you experience this first hand. How did you know all these details? I don't think it was possible for Miss Wilson to remember all these. That's why she used to take you with her and you used to write all these details and then handed over those details to Miss Wilson. I found this in Miss Wilson's study room. This is your handwriting isn't it Flora?"

Wilfred gave a piece of paper to Flora. Flora couldn't look at the paper. She was sweating.

"This is your handwriting, isn't it?" Wilfred asked again.

Flora nodded her head saying yes.

"Why didn't you tell me this before?" Wilfred asked.

"Because I was scared. I thought if I tell you all these truths, I will be in trouble. That's why I kept my mouth shut. But how did you know that is my handwriting?" Flora asked.

"You use to signature in your painting Flora. Remember I asked you is it your signature when I was watching one your paintings?" Wilfred asked.

"Yes. I do remember. So, you recognised both the handwriting?" Flora asked.

"Yes Flora. I did. So, everything I said is true right?" Wilfred asked.

"Yes" Flora said and then she asked—

"You said because of this newspaper you understood that I was the first person to discover Julia's death."

"Yes" Wilfred said.

"How?" asked Flora.

"I, Richard and Raymond were the first to get into Miss Wilson's house. But once we entered inside the house, I realised that we were not the first one. Someone had been here before us. Miss Wilson died on 15th March in between 1 to 3 AM. Because we all know that after midnight, that is after 12 it is a new day. So, it was not possible for her to get the current issue of the newspaper. But astonishingly the date of this newspaper is 15th March. Miss Wilson died way before this newspaper even reached into the hands of newspaper dealers. I don't think that newspaper dealers buy newspapers from the press in the middle of the night. Because that is when the newspapers are being printed. So, Flora, can you tell me how did this newspaper reach Miss Wilson's house after her death if someone didn't bring that there?" Wilfred stopped.

There was pin drop silence in the room.

"But I didn't know it was you until I went to your house" Wilfred said.

Flora looked at Wilfred in surprise.

"You knew Miss Wilson so closely right Flora?" Wilfred asked.

"Yes. She used to treat me as her own sister" Flora said.

"Right. So, in that case you know what she liked and disliked?" Wilfred asked.

"Of course, I did" Flora said.

"Fair enough. Then tell us Flora what newspaper Miss Wilson liked to read?" Wilfred asked.

"The Times. She loved to read The Times. I don't know why but she has a weakness towards The Times. She never liked The Herald. She used to tell me"

Flora stopped and looked at Wilfred for a few seconds and then said—

"You noticed a bunch of The Herald in my drawing room, didn't you? But you didn't find the current issue. That is how you realised that I went there before all of you came."

"Yes. I think this is what happened. Correct me if I am wrong. On 14th March Miss Wilson told you that she is going to visit the library in the night. But for some reason you couldn't go. Now if you can remember it was heavily raining on that night. So, Miss Wilson decided not to. But you didn't know that. You thought she would have gone to the library. So, you came in the morning to know what happened in the library last night. But first you went to buy the newspaper and then came to her house. You knew what time she wakes up and you also knew that Miss Wilson buys her own newspaper. That's why you just bought yours not her. I think the door was closed but not locked when you came to her house. You went inside and found Miss Wilson dead. Then you saw and read the suicide note. That's why you were so stubborn in your words that Miss Wilson didn't commit suicide. You got scared watching this and thought what if someone comes in and sees you with her dead body. So, you left the place in hurry and that's when you dropped the newspaper. But before you left you did one more thing. To make it look like nothing happened, you opened the window beside the front door from inside. Then you came out of the house and closed the door from inside by reaching the door lock through the window and then you closed the window and left. Because when we reached Miss Wilson's house, the door was closed from inside and the window wasn't locked" Wilfred stopped.

Everyone was watching Wilfred with widened eyes.

"Goodness me. Are you indwelling Mr Dankworth?" Flora asked.

"No Flora. It is just the process of detection and deduction" Wilfred said.

Wilfred waited for few minutes. Everyone was watching Wilfred with endless interest. Wilfred started talking again—

"So now the question is who murdered Miss Julia Wilson and Mr Harold Carter? To answer that we first have to think who had the better chance of killing them both. That person who knew that both Miss Wilson and Mr Carter are sticking their noses into their business. Who that person can be? Who can disappear books from the library? When I thought about this, the first thing came into my mind is that this is a work of someone from the inside of the library. Otherwise, this is not possible. Miss Wilson made the list of books that disappeared from the library. I myself have a library in my house and I am a regular reader of books. The books disappeared from the library were those books which were not that popular except one. Now it is possible for a person to know which book to steal depending on the popularity. No one will care that much because people hardly read them. But this was not possible for that person to know exactly where in the library they are kept unless that person knows the library better.

Now I told a while ago that Miss Wilson was murdered. That means she was the one who tried to stop this and came close to the truth. That's why she was murdered. So, who is that person who knows the library better? I knew who from the day one. Because I got something from Miss Wilson's house which proved me instantly that who the killer is. But I needed more proof. And to do that I set a trap. When I asked Richard who else knew about the disappearances of the books except Miss Wilson and Mr Carter, Richard said Flora Rogers."

"What? Me? You are accusing me of killing Julia? She was my sister" Flora interrupted Wilfred.

"I did not say that, Flora. Please listen me out. As I said when I asked Richard who else knew, Richard said Flora and I took that opportunity to convince both Richard and Raymond that indeed Flora Rogers killed both Julia Wilson and Harold Carter. It was very much important that they believe me. Because I knew one thing from the beginning. The murderer knew me. She knew how I work. So everywhere we went one the associate of the murderer always followed us. I so needed them to believe that I am not doubting them. Now this was easy for me act like I don't doubt them. But it was not easy for Richard and Raymond. That's why I put that idea into their mind that Flora is the killer. I also told this to Dorothy. Because she needed to know. And my plan worked. They took it lightly and walked right into my trap" Wilfred stopped for a minute and then again, he started speaking.

"I told one person that the killer left one important thing in Miss Wilson's house. I didn't have it yet but I have to get it before the killer does. I knew this would work because the killer will try to remove that from her house. And as I thought, the killer took the bet. She didn't come herself. Instead, she sent one of her associates. A man. He came around 2 AM. But he didn't know that we were waiting. He tried to run away but Richard chased him down and shot three times in his right leg. That man will never walk again. He is in hospital now. He came for this" Wilfred took out an ear ring from his pocket.

"I found this when I was searching Miss Wilson's house on the day she was murdered. Does anyone here recognise this ear ring?" Wilfred asked.

Nobody answered. But Flora was looking at that ear ring strangely.

"How is your right ear, Dorothy?" Wilfred asked in a deep cold voice.

"My ear?" Dorothy asked. She was getting agitated.

"Yes Dorothy. Your right ear. What happened?" Wilfred asked again.

"I think I told you that it was an accident" Dorothy said. She was getting angry.

"Of course, you did. Will you kindly tell me how did that happen?" Wilfred asked.

"I think I also told you that" Dorothy replied.

"But I want you to tell these people" Wilfred said.

Dorothy's face changed. She said—

"What are you trying to say?"

"Nothing Dorothy. Just tell them how did this accident happened?"

Still Dorothy kept quiet. Wilfred smiled and said—

"Can't remember what you told me. Let me help you. You said you fell down from the stairs and you right ear was smashed into the wall. Remember now?" Wilfred asked.

"You are intolerable Mr Dankworth" Dorothy's voice was getting louder. Flora couldn't believe what she was watching. Wilfred said—

"You know Dorothy, before this I never heard that someone who fell from the stairs hurt their ear instead of hurting their legs or head or hands. But unfortunately, Dorothy that wound does not look like that it was smashed on a wall. That wound is a clear indication of something sharp cut your ear. Will you kindly tell us now how your ear was cut?"

Dorothy was looking at the floor. Now she looked up. There was a clear sign of ferociousness on Dorothy's face. Then all of a sudden, she stood up and tried to take out something from her hand bag. But by the time she does that Wilfred already had his gun pointing at her.

"Seat down Dorothy. Otherwise just like your associate you too will not walk again" Wilfred said.

Dorothy sat on the couch again shivering. Wilfred said—

"Take her hand bag Raymond. She has gun inside it."

Raymond snatched Dorothy's hand bag from her. Wilfred said again—

"Now tell us how did your ear was cut?"

But Dorothy was not in the condition to talk. She opened her mouth to say something but we couldn't hear anything. Wilfred said—

"Alright Dorothy. If you can't say, then let me explain this to everyone. Miss Wilson was responsible for that wound. Because she was trying to defend herself when you and your two associates were trying to kill her by cyanide. You killed both Julia Wilson and Harold Carter in cold blood. I have enough proof and eyewitness to put you inside the prison."

"My God. Dorothy. Why?" Flora screamed.

"Because she was the master mind behind the disappearances of the books. Dorothy and her two associates are involved in smuggling jewellery out of England. They are doing this business for quite a sometimes now. They were caught once doing so but somehow Dorothy stayed away from the police. Her entire gang was caught except her. She waited for situation to calm down and then recruited only two men into her group and invented an unbelievable way to smuggle jewellery out of England. Dorothy is educated but unfortunately education could not give her wisdom. Instead, her mind always stayed on the other side of wisdom. Dorothy used her education and intelligence to find a new way of conducting business. She chose books as a cover to smuggle jewellery. Because no one will doubt books. So, she joined J.C. library. Getting that job was easy for her because she is educated. Her attentive care for the library and books earned her the trust of both Miss Wilson and Mr Carter.

Very soon both Mr Carter and Miss Wilson started to depend on her and gave her a duplicate of the master key of the library. And this is all she needed. Once she got the master key, she resumed her work again. She chose some of the unpopular books from the library so that no one will doubt. She used to make a hole in the books where she used to keep the jewellery. And as she thought, no one doubted. Once the work was done, Dorothy used to buy that same book from the shop and kept that where it was. This was going wonderfully until Miss Wilson started doubting and eventually found out about this matter. And after few months later Mr Carter also understood that books are disappearing. But he didn't know that Dorothy was the master mind behind this. So before discussing this with Miss Wilson, Mr Carter told Dorothy first about his doubt and also told that if he gets proof he may go to the police. That scared Dorothy.

But luck worked in her favour. In a small misunderstanding Mr Carter started doubting Miss Wilson and Dorothy saw that as an opportunity to remove both of them from the picture. Because I think Miss Wilson found out Dorothy is the person behind all these. So Dorothy started to make the master plan. Mr Carter already told Dorothy that he will go to the library at night. Mr Carter was very much upset because he thought her lover is doing all these. Dorothy knew Mr Carter for a long time. So, she also knew that he won't wait for a long time. So, she told one of her associates to keep an eye on Harold Carter. At 14th march, when Mr Carter went to the library, one of her associates spotted that and informed her. Dorothy on the other hand already made the plan. To make he look like Miss Wilson, she already stole Miss Wilson's dress. That dress which Mr Carter gifted to Miss Wilson. She herself stole it or maybe one of her associates did that for her.

She wore the dress and went to the library before Mr Carter reached. She spotted Mr Carter coming into the library. So, she intentionally walked in front him to prove that she is indeed Julia Wilson. Mr Carter didn't see Dorothy's face. All he saw is the dress. Dorothy then came out from the library and went exactly that way where Miss Wilson lives. Mr Carter was heartbroken and came back to his house. Dorothy and her two associates followed him. Mr Carter went inside the house and started writing the letter. Dorothy and her associates waited for few minutes and then they knocked the door. Mr Carter opened and eventually was surprised to see Dorothy on that time of the night. But Dorothy and her partners didn't wait any longer. They attacked Mr Carter and injected a needle beside his neck. Anaesthesia. Mr Carter fell in the ground and was fading away. Then most probably this is what happened. Mr Carter was lying on the floor on his back and Dorothy was seating on his chest and was trying to kill him by chocking him. Mr Carter to tried to defend himself but couldn't do a lot but somehow, he was able grab a part of Dorothy's dress and tore it. That little part of dress went under the bed which neither Dorothy nor her associates spotted. Then they searched the entire house to find that book list.

Once they got it, one of them copied Miss Wilson's handwriting and wrote the suicide note. Then they put that book list in one of Mr Carter's coat's pockets. One of the men took Mr Carter's body and went to Wiveliscombe to dump the body and Dorothy with her other associate went to Miss Wilson's house. She knocked Miss Wilson's door and might gave any excuse to get in. Once they got in, the man grabbed

Miss Wilson from behind by her throat and she went unconscious. Then both Dorothy and her associate carried her to the bed and were trying to put cyanide through her mouth. I believe that is when Miss Wilson came back to her senses and understood what was going on. She grabbed Dorothy's right ear and pulled with all the power she has and that is when the ear ring cut Dorothy's ear, fell down on the floor went under the wardrobe. But during that time the poison already went inside her mouth and started working. She couldn't fight anymore and eventually she died. But the damage had been done to Dorothy. But she held on because she had a lot of things to do.

First, she removed every document or paper which had Miss Wilson's handwriting on it. Even from the books Miss Wilson had. I and Richard checked her books personally. Some of the pages from those books were missing. This was necessary because Dorothy knew that the copy of Miss Wilson's handwriting was not an exact match. Anyone with a good detection power would have understood that. That's why she removed every document that had Miss Wilson's handwriting on it except the booklist because that would work as a proof that the both of the handwriting is same. Actually, Dorothy didn't know that someone like me who has a great detection and deduction power will investigate this case. She thought the police won't understand this small difference. After doing all of these both of them left Miss Wilson's house. But they had to stop to a petrol pump near to Miss Wilson's house because Dorothy was bleeding badly. The owner of that petrol pump is Mr David Brett. Dorothy stayed in the car and her partner came out and asked Mr Brett for bandage. Mr Brett took a little time find a bandage and necessary medication. By the time he gave the bandage to Dorothy's partner another car came to the petrol pump. That car had its headlight on and that headlight helped Mr Brett to see a woman seating in that car from where the man came out. And that woman was Dorothy. Isn't that right Mr Brett?" Wilfred asked.

"Yes Mr Dankworth. I saw her before many times with Julia. So, I knew her face. She used to come to Julia's house. So it wasn't that hard to recognise her. Though she was trying to cover her face but eventually I saw her," said Mr Brett.

We all turned towards Dorothy. Dorothy was covering her face with her two hands. Wilfred said—

"There was a lot little things which proves that Miss Wilson did not go out of her house after coming back from the library. You plan had a lot of flaws Dorothy. Your first flaw—

The distance between Miss Wilson's house and the library is quite a lot. It is not possible to cover that distance by foot. So, it is obvious that Miss Wilson always used her car to go to the library. Now if you remember Dorothy, it was raining throughout the night on 14th March. So, If Miss Wilson had taken her car, that car should have been wet because of the rain. But it wasn't. I found the car covered in cloth and that cloth was dry. Neither the car nor the cloth was wet.

And not only that, when I searched Miss Wilson's house, I didn't even get any of her dress wet. Even her umbrella and raincoat were dry. At least the raincoat should have been wet. Because it is obvious that if she really was the mastermind behind the disappearances of the books, she would never take her car near to the library for safety. Because anybody could have identified her by her car.

So, she would have done the same thing too on the night of 14th march. In that case at least her raincoat should have been wet because she had to cover a little distance in the rain by walking. But unbelievably there was nothing wet in her house. You see Dorothy, you missed out these details."

"You said there was many flaws. What are the others?" Raymond asked.

"Her second flaw was giving the responsibility to copy Miss Wilson's handwriting to that person who wrote those threat letters. The alphabet 'i' and 'p' are exactly same in both the threat letters and the suicide note. Like I said, Dorothy never thought that someone like me will investigate this case. Her third mistake was believing my words and walking right into my traps. When I spoke to Dorothy for the first time, I asked her about her ear. That's when Dorothy remembered that she had left her ear ring in Miss Wilson's house. But somehow, I made her believe that I didn't get it yet and I am not doubting her. I also told her that Flora stole Miss Wilson's dress and I believe it is still inside her house. Once I get it there will be no way out for Flora.

After hearing these words, Dorothy made another plan. She knew that the ear ring will not work in our favour because Flora will deny that this ear ring is not her. But if somehow, we get the dress, then there will be nothing to deny. Now that dress was in Dorothy's house. I didn't know that for sure but I guessed and took a chance.

I told Raymond to watch Dorothy's house last night. Because Dorothy will take this opportunity to plant the dress into Flora's house. And she tried. She sent her other associate to get the job done and this is when he was caught red handed with the dress. That dress has a little part missing. In that same night Richard shot down Dorothy's other associate at Chiswell Street." Wilfred said and then showed the dress to all of us.

Indeed, there was a part missing. Dorothy started to cry. Wilfred said—

"Your fourth mistake was telling me that Mr Carter went to the library and gone missing. Do you remember that, Dorothy? You said that you had no idea that Mr Carter would take a drastic step like this and will go to the library. How did you know that he went to the library on 14th march in the night? You left his house in the evening. You also told me and the police that he went missing from last night. How did you know that he went missing from the last night? He could have gone missing from the morning. You know Dorothy, there is a saying. Too much cunning overreaches itself. You tried to be cleaver. And in doing so you gave me information unknowingly.

You fifth mistake was filing a missing person report too early to the police without even looking into those places where Mr Carter can go. You opened the library at 10 AM. That's what you told the police. And at 11 AM you filed the missing person's report. I never saw in my life that if a person goes missing for an hour someone flies a missing person's report because that person is missing for an hour. When I asked you that did Miss Wilson know that Mr Carter is missing, you said no. That means you didn't go to her house to check whether Mr Carter was there or not. He could have been there. But you didn't check. Wow Dorothy. You killed two wonderful souls who used to love each other. Miss Wilson did decide to marry Mr Carter. She told this to Mr Brett only. She was waiting for this problem to be solved. And you took them away from this world. I don't think God will ever forgive you Dorothy."

"Julia was about to marry Mr Carter? But she never told this to me" Flora said with a lot of surprise.

"Yes Flora. Only Mr Brett knew. Mr Brett loved Miss Wilson as his own daughter and Miss Wilson also loved and respected Mr Brett as her father. That's why she told her. Anyway, my job is done here. Take her away Raymond" Wilfred said.

Raymond and four constable hand cuffed Dorothy and took her away. Mr Brett came towards Wilfred and said—

"Thank you, son. You gave my daughter and Mr Carter justice. I will pray to Lord Jesus to give both of their souls an eternal peace."

"We will do the same Mr Brett. We will go back to Wiveliscombe tonight. Stay safe Mr Brett" Wilfred said.

I was looking at Wilfred. He asked—

"What?"

"Nothing. I think I was wrong in one thing" I said.

"What?" he asked.

"You do understand what love is all about. Because you felt for both Miss Wilson and Mr Carter" I said.

Wilfred smiled and said "Let's go home Richard. A new tune came into my mind. I have to compose this as soon as possible. Otherwise, it will go out from my head."

About the Author

Satanik Basu

Satanik Basu, a post graduate in Computer Science and Application and a guitarist by profession was born in 1st February 1989 in Kolkata, India. His love for books began when he was 12 years old. Detective, crime and thriller became his favourite genres and still are now. His first ever book was published in the International Kolkata Book fair 2022 under the publication house "The Cafe Table", a Kolkata based publisher. The book was based on thriller and mystery. The language of the book was Bengali. He also participated in a creative writing competition where I ranked 50 in the country.

www.ingramcontent.com/pod-product-compliance
Lightning Source LLC
LaVergne TN
LVHW041942070526
838199LV00051BA/2872